IN THE HOUSE UPON THE DIRT BETWEEN

SOHO

THE LAKE AND THE WOODS

MATT BELL

Published by
Soho Press, Inc.
853 Broadway
New York, NY 10003

Library of Congress Cataloging-in-Publication Data is available.

ISBN 978-1-61695-253-2
eISBN 978-1-61695-254-9

Interior design by Janine Agro, Soho Press, Inc.

Printed in the United States of America

10 9 8 7 6 5 4 3 2 1

In memory of John Schantz, uncle and friend and teacher

It seems likely that there are but two and that these beget no offspring, for I believe it is always the same ones that appear.

— *The King's Mirror*

TRANSLATED BY LAURENCE MARCELLUS LARSON

1

BEFORE OUR FIRST ENCOUNTER WITH the bear I had already finished building the house, or nearly so.

In the hasty days that followed, I feared we moved in too
fast and too early, the house's furnishings still incomplete, the
doors not all right-hinged—and in response to my worries my
wife said that was no trouble, that she could quickly finish what I
had mostly made.

Beneath the unscrolling story of new sun and stars and then-
lonely moon, she began to sing some new possessions into the
interior of our house, and between the lake and the woods I heard
her songs become something stronger than ever before. I returned
to the woods to cut more lumber, so that I too might add to our
household, might craft for her a crib and a bassinet, a table for
changing diapers, all the other furnishings she desired. We labored
together, and soon our task seemed complete, our house readied
for what dreams we shared—the dream I had given her, of family, of husband and wife, father and mother, child and child—and
when the earliest signs of my wife's first pregnancy came they
were attended with joy and celebration.

T HE DIRT'S WETTEST SEASON SWELLED, and then its hottest burst the world to bloom, and through those tumid months my wife swelled too, expanded in both belly and breast until the leaves fell—and afterward came no more growth, only some stalling of the flesh gathering within her. Even before it was obvious that there would be no baby, even then my wife began to cry, to sing sadder songs that dimmed our already-fuel-poor gas-lamps, or cracked cups and bowls behind cupboard doors.

I angered that we would have to start again, and if my wife was not to birth some son then I wished only for that pregnancy's speedy end, so that she might not suffer overlong, so that another child might be put in this one's place. But still her body delayed, pretending that the bundle inside her might grow into some child, and my wife pretended too, and when I could not stand her insistence I again went out back of the house to where my wife had planted a garden, some few tubers and herbs to supplement what fish I took daily from the lake.

Now in my frustration I returned that place to the dirt it had been, and later my wife confronted me with what I had done. Her anger flushed her face, and her yelling contained none of the music I loved in her singing voice, and as she exhausted her still-round shape of its rage then at last I saw her labor was upon us.

What sad and sorry shape was born from her after those next days, that labor made long despite the lack of life within:

Not an arm, but an arm bud. Not a leg, but a leg bud, a proto-knee.

Not a heart but a heart bulge.

Not an eye but an eye spot, half covered by a translucent lid, uselessly clear.

Not a baby, instead only this miscarriage, this finger's length of intended and aborted future.

And what was not born: No proper umbilical cord snaked from mother to baby, from placenta to belly, and so the starved child passed from my wife's body into a clot of blood and bedsheet, and then into my waiting hand, where I lifted it before my eyes to look upon its wronged shape, that first terminus of my want.

Then to my lips, as if for a single kiss, hello and goodbye.

Then no kiss at all, but something else, some compulsion that even then I knew was wrong but could not help, so strong was my sadness, so sudden my desire: Into my body I partook what my wife's had rejected, and while she buried her face in the red ruin of our blankets I swallowed it whole—its ghost and its flesh small enough to have in my fist like an extra finger, to fit into my mouth like an extra tongue, to slide farther in without the use of teeth—and I imagined that perhaps I would succeed where she had failed, that my want for family could again give our child some home, some better body within which to grow.

What was there to say afterward, when my wife returned to her senses, when she asked to hold our dead child? What else to tell but that our child was gone: that while she screamed out her frustration I had taken the body to the lake, that I had set it to float away on waters safer than those red waves at drift within her body.

When her howls subsided, her voice was made different than ever before: There was still some baby inside her, she said, some better other that she might bring forth, and so she worried at the entrance to her womb, first with her fingers and then, later, with tools made for other tasks, until all the bedding was mucked with her. I tried to take these implements from her hands, but with increasing ferocity she shoved me back, with the balls of her freed fists, and with a song that staggered me from the bedside, her new voice climbing, hurling strange my name and the name we had meant for our child. In rising verses, she demanded I disappear, leave her, throw myself into the depths of the salt-soaked lake, cast my now-unwanted bones after the supposed casting of our stillbirth, that failure-son.

Drown yourself away, my wife sang, and then despite my want to stay I found myself again outside the house, for against the fury of her song my horror held neither strength nor will nor strategy.

Across the dirt, upon a dock I had built with my own hands, the wind and the rain fell upon my face and the face of the lake, and there I felt the first stirrings of the fingerling, as that swallowed son would come to be called, by me and me alone:

A child or else the ghost of a child, clenched inside my chest, swam inside my stomach, nestled inside my ear.

A minnow or a tadpole, a tapeworm or a leech.

A listener. A whisperer.

A voice, louder without vocal cords.

A voice: FATHER, FATHER, FATHER.

FATHER and FATHER and FATHER.

FATHER, FATHER, a title repeated over and over, until I began to believe: no longer merely a husband, but something more.

And yet I hid this new self, did not confess what I had done when later my wife limped outside, her slender fingers pressing a rag bloody between her impatient legs as she walked down the hill to where I stood sullen upon the dock, to where she opened her mouth to speak, then shut it in silence, then opened it again: a show of teeth, her hesitant tongue, the animal of her grief.

At last she made those shapes to move about the wording of her demand, asking that I take her out onto the lake, where she had never before wanted to go.

Take me where you took him, she said. And what else was there but to agree, to show her the place where my lie had drawn her thoughts, her sorrow's desire.

The gray lake was motioned only momentarily by our presence upon its sluggish waters, its surface rippled with wind and dashed by my oars but headed always for another flatness, another deeper kind of floating quiet, stiller still, and there was our boat atop it as night fell, as the sky filled with moon and stars and the absence of nearer light. Only then did my wife stand in the rowboat, her movements sudden, unannounced. I worked to steady the boat and so did not grasp her intent when she began to sing, for the first time using her voice not to create or cast up shapes but to take them down — and how could I have even hoped to stop such a power?

With song after song, with a song for each of their names, my wife lured some number of the stars one by one from out the sky, and those so named could not resist her call. Their lights dropped and crashed all around us, nearly upon us, and though they dimmed as they fell, still they landed too bright for our smaller world, and I shielded my face against the flash of their collisions, then covered my ears against the booming that followed. Those that slipped into the water splashed and steamed, and over the rocking edge of the boat I watched queasily as their hot lights dropped, until I lost them into the depths. Where they struck the dirt they did more damage, their fire scorching soil to sand to glass, and then in the growing darkness and the fading light the rain continued until the last fallen stars were extinguished.

Back onshore, I lifted my wife out of the boat's flooding bottom and onto the dock, and how easy a burden she was then. I cradled her exhausted limpness, held her to my chest as I had hoped that night to hold a child, and in this way we climbed up the path from the lake, across the burned and muddy and darkened dirt, then into the false refuge of the house, where in those unlit rooms our new future awaited to tempt us into trying again: for the family we still hoped to make, the family for which my wife was again scraped ready, made to possess some hungry space, some hollow as full of want as my own hard gut had always been.

O N THE DAY OF OUR wedding, on some now-distant beach, my wife had sworn herself to me with ease and in faith, and I did likewise for her: Together we made the longest promises, vowed them tight, and it was so easy to do this then, to speak the provided words, when we did not know what other harder choices would necessarily follow as we made our first life together in a new city, and then again after we left that country and journeyed to the dirt, this plot stationed so far from the other side of the lake, from the mountains beyond the lake, on whose distant slopes we had once dwelled in the land of our parents, where perhaps there still perches that platform where we stood to speak our vows.

How terrible we must have seemed that day, when together we were made to believe our marriage would then and always be celebrated, by ceremony and by feasting, by the right applause of a hundred kith and kin. And then later how we were terrible again, upon this far lonelier shore, where when we came we came alone.

When we first arrived upon the dirt between the lake and the woods, then there was still sun and moon, only one moon, and stars too, all the intricacies of their intersections circumscribing the sky, their paths a tale to last every night, a waking dream to fill the hours of every day, and despite that bounty my wife was often flush with tears, because what world we had found was not enough for her, not enough for me, not without the children we desired, that I desired and that she desired for me, and despite her doubts she said that she would try, if that was what I assured her I wished.

In those days, there was no house, and until there was we required some place to sleep, to store the many objects we had been gifted at our wedding, the others we had carried forward from other years, those lived beneath the auspices of our mothers and fathers. And so we went into the woods to seek a cave, and in a cave we laid out our blankets and stacked our luggage, and there my wife waited amid that piled potential while each day I went out onto the dirt, while I raised a house with just my shovel and axe, my hammer and saw, my hands hardened by the same.

In that cave I did not leave her alone, though I had meant to do so — and all this happened long ago, when I still thought meaning to do something was the same as doing it — and I too was lonely as I built the house, and then the first rough shapes inside. I built the table and chairs, fashioned the stove and the sink, crafted the bed where I would lay my wife the first night I brought her across the threshold: where as I watched, the ink of her hair wrote one future after another across the pillows and sheets, and in that splay of black on white I smiled to see all the many possibilities of our family, formed out of her body, drawn into my arms.

But first another memory, the day before I carried my wife into our house, the other reason she was in my arms, the first time I spied the bear watching me from within its woods: And when I saw it I stilled my work upon the dirt, moved slowly to set down the tools with which I had not quite completed the house. At the tree line that marked the edge of the woods the giant bear's back hackled, increased its size again, and the wedge of its head swayed huge and square from its massive shoulders, its mouth spilling yellowed teeth and lolling tongue, exhalations steaming the morning chill. In the face of its stare, I stared back, and the bear slavered in response, shook its thick fur as welcome or warning, and when it saw it had my attention it stood on its huge hind legs, its stamping body a dark tower opening, opening to push a roar up toward the heavens, toward the sun that in those days still ran full circle.

I froze, afraid the bear would charge, and in my fear I for a breath forgot my wife; and in the next breath I remembered, flushed with the shame of that forgetting.

The bear growled and raked the ground and paced the tree line. From my remove I noted the strangeness of its rankled movement and also how it was not exactly whole: where brown fur should have covered the expanse of its back, that fur was in places ripped, and the skin below was torn so that an armor of bone poked through the wound, yellowed and slickly wet. Still the bear seemed hardly to know its hurt, its movements easy, unslowed, perhaps untinged with pain. It roared, roared again, then abruptly it returned to the pathless woods, its bounding passage wide but somehow also impossible to track, the bear tearing no new way, breaking no brambles despite the bulk of its body.

And then I too was running into and through the woods by my own path, across the avenues of pine straw, back to where I had left her, the cave where all our possessions were stored.

I arrived to find our crates and cargo shattered upon the cave's floor, our clothes shredded, our clock broken, our wedding albums ripped from their bindings. With the passing of those photos went some memories of the old world across the lake, a place perhaps already doomed to fade soon after our arrival in this new one, but now lost before I had erected the structures necessary to withstand that loss, and still some more terrible fear welled large within me, because despite my many cries my wife did not make herself known, and so for some time I did not know if she was alive or dead.

When I finally found her, sequestered in the entranceway of some lower passage of the cave I had never before seen, then as I shook her awake I saw there was no recognition in her dazed eyes, not of who I was to her or who she was to me. She did not know even the single syllable of her name, nor the two of mine, not until I repeated those sounds for her—and then I made her to say them back, to name me her husband, herself again my wife.

T HE FINGERLING DID NOT VACATE my body as all other meat had. Instead he founded new residencies, new homes different from the womb he had previously inhabited, when his trajectory was pathed toward a more ordinary existence, that series of hatchings and moltings, egg to fetus to baby, boy to man. Now he was only this dead thing, ghosted into my belly-hole, into my lungs and my thigh, and in his first years he remained the pointer, so that he might one day notice my failings, and also the indexer, so that even from his earliest moments he might catalogue their occurrence. In both shapes he often revealed what he said my wife was doing wrong, and so began the long road of my turn against her, a difference from our recent past, where in my more temporary angers I had only turned away.

Accompanied by her sighs and her songs, my wife spent the dark months of that winter wandering the house, filling the then-few rooms with the detritus of her desires, opening and closing and shaping her mouth to call them forth, shaping new sounds into new words, into shapes that contained those words and sounds, and despite the scraped wound between her legs—that constant ooze of blood that for a time left her skin paled even whiter than before—still she sang into being these inscrutable objects, a table stained with molasses, a basket of hard fruits, a crib stinking with spilt milk, as sour smelling as what leaked from her still-expectant breasts, her body that had not yet admitted its loss.

In the kitchen she hung a wall with spoons as shiny as the star-flashed glass that pocked the dirt, then filled a cupboard with matching sets of bowls, each the size of her two cupped hands. Soon I found her also revisiting the furnishings I had made for the fingerling, and as I trailed her through our rooms she sang a song over their forms, taking the rude shapes I had made and adding to their naked function some flourishes, prettifications: Now the bassinet was filigreed with ornate leaves, now the changing table was guarded on each corner not by a simple post but by a wooden bird as detailed as any ever born from egg.

Everything I made she improved, but it was not improvement I craved, only title, control, mastery. Always I had planned to be the maker of things, a steward of artifice, and yet here she was, able to call from within what I had to cull from without. In my anger I tested her powers, asked her to make some varied objects that I desired for the house, certain tools and utensils harder to craft, and when those requests did not defeat her expanded ability, then I asked for something else, something just for me: some amount of steel, fashioned into traps, a complement to my fishing tackle, the tools of my previous employment, with which I might perhaps venture into the woods, after the fur of small animals I had seen living under those trees.

My wife frowned but did not deny me, for in those days we refused each other nothing. She created and created, and when I could not abide any more of her objects—shapes meant for a once-expected childhood, now only mocking, robbed of any right utility—then I began to take more of my hours outside the house I had built, inhabiting instead the lake and the woods, whose strange failings could not be laid so squarely upon my deeds, nor the body of my wife.

And yet for a long time after their making I delayed putting my traps to work, because it was fishing for which I was best built. The lake was thick with salt and did not freeze, and that first winter I took only such numbers as were necessary for our table, lured the lake's silver swimmers from the depths with hook and line, with wriggling bait and heavy sinkers. In those days, the fingerling did not often speak—he was still in his infancy, and even as a ghost there was perhaps some semblance of rules, progressions—but upon the lake he stirred, swimming throughout the channels of my body more easily than when my feet were planted upon dry land. Between casts, I placed my palm up under the blousing of my shirt, probed for his presence, and as the fingerling left his hole in my belly to swim against my surface I was more easily able to learn his movements, often swift beneath my skin, and also the peculiar numbness that accompanied his too-long presence in one organ or another, as if my senses had been sundered, as if it was his will my body spoke to then, instead of my own.

It was only this first child that I swallowed, secreted away, and by the time the fingerling had wintered within me for several years, in between had come and passed some other brothers who did not take, some sisters whose cells refused my wife's bloody chamber. With each of their passings my wife made again the angry words I did not want her to have to speak, and then again there was her

bloodied dress dragged into the yard, again my begrudged rowing her out upon the lake, again the calling down of the stars by
the strength of her song, its harsh syllables always sung after we
let float away the body of some newest child, so unprepared
we could hardly call it stillborn.

At last the sky was so dimmed and emptied of its ancient alphabet
that we lost the shapes of even the oldest stories, the comforts of
our parents' myths, for now there was no more sky-bear, no tall-
tree beside it or gold-crown to rest upon its head, and also no more
lake-whale or salt-squid hanging in the sea of stars above the dirt.
From then on whatever sky we lived beneath was not the sky of our
parents, and whatever stories we might tell our children would not
be the stories we had been told.

Now the fingerling came into possession of his full voice, and
often he whispered darkly in my ear, revealing the objects my
wife sang into being but then hid or else buried: the mismatched
booties hidden beneath the bed, long after she had promised to
stop their creation; the tiny bonnets hanging behind her own in
the closet; the dresses made for the late maternity she had not yet
had, their austere fabrics meant to drape over the swollen object of
those expectant months.

Out back of the house, the fingerling showed me the first
bassinet, the one I had made and that she had improved, now
broken and buried beneath the nightshade, the monkshood, the
pennyroyal—and then he asked what it was my wife intended
to grow, knowing I had no answer for his smirking question.
Already I was made to learn to despise him by his words, and
also sometimes her, and as each child sputtered inside her, my
wife moved away, or else I did, until at last we were rarely in

the same part of the house, our voices kept too distant to easily speak to each other.

It was only then that I first saw what else the fingerling had been trying to show me: the newly variable nature of our rooms, of the house that contained them, and how my wife's rolling apart in the night tore away more than just the blankets. As her side of our bedchamber grew some few inches, I did what little I could to right our arrangement, tugged hard at the blankets that barely covered the widened bed — until again all things were distributed evenly, even as they were somehow also farther apart.

THERE WAS FRESH JOY IN my wife's voice when she announced the beginning of her last pregnancy, and in the weeks that followed some same feeling of hope came to inhabit my own chest-space, as if after so much disappointment I could so easily be filled with love for this child she claimed was better coming. Buoyed by her words, our best marriage resumed: We began again to eat together, at noon and at dusk, our fish filleted and fried upon our plates, garnished with vegetables from her garden. Each evening we met in our sitting room to read the scattered, unordered pages of our few remaining books, and then at night we lay side by side, bodies close but always not touching — as then I believed her delicate, capable of being disturbed from her pregnancy — and also that our next child was just as fragile, some uneasy swimmer in danger of being jostled from out her body, as all his lake-bound brothers and sisters had been, as the fingerling had before them.

After my wife had remained pregnant for a full season, then she took me by the hand, pulled me up from my chair and out onto the dirt beyond the front porch, into the place where the dirt had become most glassed, most reflective of what sun and moon shone upon it. There my wife again began to sing, and with some new song—one more powerful than any other I had yet heard or imagined—she took something from me, and also a similar portion from herself, and into the sky she lifted what she had taken until it took on some enlarged shape, until it became a heavenly body with its own weight and rotation and orbit: At the request of her melody, our flesh became a new moon, a twin to the one already hung.

Beneath its new light, my wife explained that her moon was a shape meant not to reveal the sky but perhaps to split the dirt, to destroy what house I had built, its shifting walls. Not a memorial to her sorrow, but at last a way to end it: With the crashing shatter of the moon, the lake would empty its waters, and the woods would burst into flame, and even the cities across the far mountains might shake with the horror of our divorce. The moon would someday fall—this she promised, regardless of her pregnancy's outcome, for the sky was not made to hold its weight—but with song she could delay its plummet into the far future, for the sake of this new joy in her belly.

And if there was no child coming, only another in our line of small disasters?

My wife's smile broadened, so wide that for the first time in many years I spied a certain number of her backmost teeth, her pinkest gums, and then she said, I have grown so weary of these many beginnings, and it is only endings that I still crave, only middles I might agree to bear.

W E HAD NEVER BEFORE EATEN meat, only fish, but the woods in those years brimmed with life, and at my wife's request I began to trap that bounty, so I might bring home new sustenance for her table, so that she might make the furs into blankets meant to keep her warm while she grew this best last chance of a child. But the smell of seared rabbit or boiled squirrel turned my stomach, and I could not be made to try it, preferring instead the catch from the gray waters of the lake. My wife had no such hesitation, and so took apart whatever I found with fork and knife, with savage fingers tearing seared muscle into smaller bites fit for her greased lips. I faced into her new gluttony, its sight offending from across the table, and at the fingerling's suggestion I asked her why she needed these new foods, this meat that came to displace fish and fruit and vegetable until all her diet was red and bloodied, as never it had been before.

In my father's house, she said, we ate only fish, but I am no longer in my father's house, and the old ways no longer bind me.

She slid her pooled plate toward me, said that in this small world there were pleasures and powers I had not yet imagined and that through them we might find some strength to share.

She said, Together we will remake this dirt, the sky above it and the ground below, and all the animals and birds and fish that crawl and fly and swim upon and around it, and by our own new laws we will be better married, made anew.

A family, she said. What you have always wanted, at last arrived; for one way or another, I have found the will to give it.

I did not know then of what she spoke, was afraid of this new manner in her speech, its sound so like my own worst thoughts, like those of the fingerling. And so I shook my head, asked her not to speak this way again, and after she withdrew her plate I returned to the woods, where afterward I spent more and more of my time.

In my absence, my wife filled our rooms with more new-sung objects, baby-things for her baby, made this time from no template of mine but rather out of her own imagining. Meanwhile I turned my anger to task as I worked to empty the woods of all the animals favored by the bear, who I came to believe was lord over that shaded domain.

When I say *belief*, I do not mean I knew what I believed, not in the way I had believed before coming to the dirt, in steepled buildings made to organize such feelings. Things were odder here than they were elsewhere, and most stories were not written as clearly: On the other side of the lake, across the mountains, the truth had been inscribed in the stars and could not be changed. Here, upon the dirt, my wife had wiped clean that sky-flung slate, and so I was not sure what to believe or where to look to rediscover what once I had simply known.

Throughout this pregnancy's middle months, the fingerling and I continued to trap the woods, to bring home what meat and furs we earned. Our nights stretched troubled, some feeling in the gut appearing in my dreams as in the fingerling's, its shadow disrupting our sometimes-blended nightscapes with unsure worries. From within those sleepless hours I would emerge blearily from the house, returning to the woods to check my traps for ferret or fox, for the rabbits or wild hounds stuck in the steel jaws of my mechanisms, and because I did not know what else to do with those whose meat she refused, I took up the taxidermist's craft, the tanner's: To skin, to scrape, to preserve the furs. To make my wife shut them with needle and thread, for when our first clothes had turned to rags. To reclaim them as memory, their bodies arranged with glue and wire, their skins stretched over wood forms meant to decorate the walls of our house, to displace the long-empty picture frames.

Above the traps, where shafts of moonlight descended through the boughs, often a space existed wherein some segment of the shifted sky could be seen, where the last stars remaining did not retain their original seats but rather slid along new curves, their paths distorting as the second moon's weight tugged the sky. Each night the fingerling catalogued this movement, and together my eager watcher and I searched for other signs, like how the once-white glow of my wife's moon was perhaps even then tinged some shade of pink, and the sky was not all we watched, nor all we wondered about. More and more, we pondered what my wife learned in the cave, that house of the bear, when we lived there without knowing to whom the cave belonged: How long did she know about the bear before it awoke from its long sleep?

How long did my wife know, and what did she find between the time of her first knowing and that awakening, the bear rising to chase her from its home?

Whatever she found, was this the source of her stronger songs, of the voice that made her words more powerful than mine, even though it was I who had claimed this dirt to rule? Or was it something else, something she and I had done together?

That was the question I worried at, that I gnawed at like a bone, a cast-off rib too stubborn to share its marrow. And when at last that bone broke, what truth escaped its fracture, was by it remade: for even our bones had memories, and our memories bones.

L ATER MY WIFE LEFT FOR the woods too, perhaps for the first time since our fleeing the cave of the bear in our earliest, more innocently childless days: I knew only that first she was beside me in our bed, and then she was gone, into a night lengthened beyond reason; and though I did not sleep, I pretended to, so that when her absence ended she would not have to explain. I trusted her then as I would not trust her later, not even early that next morning, when upon her return and her resumption of sleep—and also time, I thought then, oddly—the fingerling seized the dawn-light's warm chance to show how it was not just mud that caked brown my wife's heels and ankles. And still I refused to see what I was shown, even as the fingerling urged me toward right thinking.

I did not want to do what he claimed was necessary, to lift my wife's nightclothes and confirm the new stains streaking dark her white thighs, and while the fingerling begged me to show him, to show us, I told him I would not push my wife farther into this misery, would not compound her sadness with the forced and early addition of my own.

I watched my sleeping wife, hovered my hand over the scroll of her hair. And to the fingerling, I said, Wait.

Wait, I said.

Wait until she awakens.

Wait until she washes and eats.

Wait until she has readied herself with freshest clothing, until her hair is returned to its bindings, until her face is rouged and powdered. Then she will tell us all we need to know: what has happened, what will happen next, and when at last it will all be over.

M Y WIFE EMERGED FROM OUR bedchambers late, as was her cus-
tom throughout those childless years.

Dressed only in her nightclothes, ankles stained, she
walked through the kitchen and out the front door to the dirt
beyond, while I sat at our slab of table with my fork and my fish,
while in my half-filled stomach the fingerling looped anxious
orbits. He begged me to follow her onto the porch or at least to spy
upon her through some opened window, yet I maintained what
slim calm lingered — for if my wife's pregnancy had truly ended —
if our last good chance had indeed passed unborn between her
legs — then she had promised to end our world, then surely that
end was come.

But then morning passed into day into evening into night.

I listened, but the song did not come, the calling-down sung
after each of her other pregnancies, and when at last I opened
the door, there was no wife out upon the dirt, or near the lake,
or in the woods, no matter how or where I searched: Again she
had disappeared from the surface of all things, just as she had

the day the bear destroyed our wedding gifts at the mouth of its cave.

When at last she returned, her pregnancy seemed not ended, despite the grief bloodshot through her eyes, the stagger pained into her step. I asked her where she had gone and what she had done, but she said only that she was tired, that she did not wish to speak. Her body betrayed none of the quick deflation it had before, and so I did not know what to say or do, and afterward I kept some distance during the day and also in the night, and I gave her more than her share of what I trapped and fished, so that she might feed this baby better, so that if it were somehow still within her it might find the strength to live.

From that night on, my wife avoided our bed, sleeping instead alone upon the dirt, beneath the moon and also her moon, bidding me not to follow but to promise to remain inside the house — and even though I promised, my promise was not enough.

Each evening I again agreed to retire to the bedchamber, agreed as if I had never been asked, my wife's voice betraying no recognition of our patterns, of my nightly exile to our lonely bed, where only the fingerling's terrors would keep me company.

Then my wife saying good night, muffled through the closing and closed door.

Then the key moving in the lock.

Then the latch making it easy not to break my promise.

Then the waiting until dark, until the darker dark inside, and then moving to the window, where I believed I would not be seen.

From that vantage, I could not spy where she lay, but I could hear her voice, and as I listened she filled the nights with a song she had not sung before, the purpose of which I could not divine.

Each morning, she returned at dawn in her draped and dirtied nightgown to unlock the bedchamber door, and no matter what she said I did not question her, only chose to believe the best of the many possibilities, that her acned skin and ruddied cheeks and heavied body were some good sign, some assurance that this pregnancy continued, that there was still some child coming. This was the story I wanted most, and so it was easiest to believe, no matter what the fingerling claimed — and also there was the matter of her moon, neither ascending nor descending. If her pregnancy had ended, then I thought there would be no need for these locked doors, these separate nights, not against the language of her eyes, the promised danger of her sung moon.

In my hopeful naïveté I made believe that the moon's place in the sky assumed or assured a child's place in her, but while I slept the fingerling begged my eyes open, watching and waiting and never allowing me to forget what we had seen, that night my wife had returned bloodied to the bed.

YOU KNOW THERE IS NO CHILD, the fingerling said, his shape curled in upon my ear, circling its ugly organ with each word, each soft-slung syllable. THERE IS ONLY A LIE, WHICH IN YOUR WEAKNESS YOU ALLOW HER TO KEEP, TO HOLD AGAINST YOU.

EXPOSE HER, he said, and then he slipped his shape across my face, around the curve of my jawline, down into the spiral canals of my other ear, crowding that too-small space so that he might command my attention, so that he might speak longer than he had spoken before: EXPOSE HER AND MAKE HER PAY. FOR HER DECEPTION, FOR WHAT SHE DID TO YOU, FOR WHAT SHE DID TO ME, TO MY OTHER BROTHERS AND SISTERS.

He said, I HAVE SEEN THE INSIDE OF HER SHAPE, AS I HAVE SEEN THE INSIDE OF YOURS, AND I TELL YOU IT IS NOT OUR LACK BUT HERS.

Despite the tickle of the fingerling in and around my face, still I dissented. Long had I saddened at the failure of my children, at the ghost I had set to seed, but never had I blamed my wife, not in full, not as we expanded the distance between our bodies, not after we had ceased to smile at each other in doorways or through windows. Some part of that distancing had been reversed by this pregnancy, and in this last-found closeness I wanted to believe all the fingerling claimed I should not; and even if her pregnancy was over, then perhaps I was willing to blame her actions on the twisting unreasonableness of heartbreak, and so I did not agree that my wife had done me wrong.

Against these arguments the fingerling insisted, and in my refusal of that insistence the fingerling showed me some others of his tricks, demonstrated how he too was a tracker. He had learned his mother's movements, and also her motives, knew both better than I ever had, and so one hot afternoon he urged me back to the house, hurried me until I abandoned my shouldered burden to walk faster: For weeks, my wife had sung upon the dirt throughout the darkest hours while in the locked bedchamber I slept or tried to sleep. Now she was too exhausted to resist napping some portion of the day, and so the fingerling commanded me to tread lightly, to open the front door without creaks, to cross the floorboards without boots, to enter the bedroom, to see there what might be seen.

LIFT HER SHIRT, bid the fingerling, hysterical, foamed and frothed, a nausea of need, and I did as he begged, and beneath my wife's blouse I found what he wanted me to find: a fur, balled into the shape and size of a baby's bulge; this hide with which my wife had hoped to deceive me, as if our son was to be a wolf, as if she had last rucked with an animal.

WAKE HER, the fingerling commanded, but I did not wake her.

WAKE HER, the fingerling said again, but it was only the fingerling who was angry then, only he who wanted her so quickly exposed and punished. For my part, there was almost only more sadness, that she could not admit what had happened, this expulsion from her body of our most recent child, which unlike all the others she had delivered dead alone.

NOW CAME THE MONTHS OF crossed deceptions, where we each hid beneath our clothes some child or not-child, grown inside our bodies or else never grown: For me there was the fingerling, five years swallowed, willful, angered at what world he knew only through me, his father-shaped host; and for my wife there was her own false child, her lie made artifact, a fakery of fur clutched always under her blouses and dresses.

Despite this gathering evidence, I did not call my wife's bluff, only counted the days and weeks and months as they passed. Each night, after I was locked into our bedchamber, there I scratched a new mark into the floor beneath the bed, some reminder of the length of her deception, a predictor of its likely end, a calendar made more necessary as the season stalled, so that often it was the cloudless distress of winter, the harsh light of sun and moons cold despite the sometimes-bright blue of the sky.

Whenever we snuck into the house during her nap to lift her shirt, to spy again her deception, always her body appeared pregnant everywhere but her belly, where there were always only the bundled furs between her shirt and her flat skin, and no baby besides, and no matter the strength of her songs I did not then believe those furs would ever become a baby, even as she otherwise remained seemingly with child, heavy-breasted, thick-thighed. And so in the ninth month I emerged unsuspecting from the woods, still merely a husband, made no proper father despite the insistent promises of my wife, the hungry claims of the fingerling upon my flesh.

That day, I felt myself only a fisherman, only a trapper with rabbits in hand, but already I had been remade again, my station changed upon an event unattended and now revealed: In our sitting room, in the rocking chair I had hewn for the fingerling's birth, there my wife waited holding a baby boy, his wide face howling, his wrinkled body swaddled into some blanket I had never seen, perhaps also only lately sung into being.

Memory as new fatherhood's first failing: To have my wife stand and pass the baby's warm weight into my arms, then with a whisper press the child's name against my ears. To hold the happy shape of this son and for a moment not care where he came from, not care how he was made, not care that in my joy I was believing what did not deserve belief—and then to have this feeling taken as the fingerling reacted, attacked, punched out from within the cage of my ribs until my heart thumped wrong, until I stumbled and reeled, until my horrified wife reclaimed the baby from my embrace before I could drop him to the floor.

YOU WILL NEVER LOVE HIM, said the fingerling. I WILL NEVER ALLOW IT. THIS BROTHER, YOU WILL NEVER KEEP HIM CLOSE AS YOU HAVE KEPT ME, AND ALWAYS I WILL CLAIM YOU FOR MYSELF—

Is this not what you wanted? asked my wife. Have I not given you what you asked of me, all you have ever asked?

No matter which way I opened my mouth, I did not know what

to say, how to say anything without saying it all. Against my unexplained distance my wife clutched tighter this foundling, the baby boy whom she called our son, whom she called a name meant for another, for one of our previous failed children. With the boy held to her breasts, now suckling oblivious, then my wife insisted again that this was my child, that I should not doubt, that she did not understand why I doubted.

She smiled and said, We made this child together, with one body woven against the other, as we had tried to make so many others.

At my silence she tried again to smile, and I tried too, and when I failed I left behind that joy and confusion to step out onto the porch, then onto the dirt, where in private I might let my body shake. I circled round behind the house, and there I discovered the garden already unmade, its dank sod overturned, the many buried objects of baby raising now ripped anew from its earth so that they might be reinstalled in the house, each useful at last.

And then to have to look back at the house I had built, filled now with what I had not.

To have to listen to the fingerling say, I TOLD YOU SO, I TOLD YOU I TOLD YOU SO.

To have to have him be right, and to not yet know what that meant.

MY WIFE, HOLDING HER NEWBORN, her body taking full part in her false motherhood, so that her breasts were ample in the months after the finding, and at her tit seemingly always the foundling nursed, drinking deep: I rarely held him myself, but from across our rooms I measured his quality, surveyed his coarse black hair, his wide face and heavy-lidded eyes, the warm bulge of his plumped belly and limbs, his mouth that could then make only the dumbest sounds, cries announcing hunger, exhaustion, a soiling. It was a son I had wanted and a son I had been given, but what son was this? Even in his infancy I recoiled at how possessive his crinkled fingers were, holding her to his lips with more urgency than those of any baby I'd known, more than any of the right-born sons I'd seen on the other side of the lake, the first objects of my bachelor's jealousy. Still I was not satisfied, and I was not alone in the anger I felt, my strange rejection of the baby's health, the baby: Ghosted within my belly, the fingerling swam faster to make his own feelings known, stung his renewed need throughout his home of bile and half-digested fish, where in the absence of his mother's milk he had found some fair substitute, so that by then he had surely devoured some permanent part of me; not what I made with my body, but what my body was made of.

FOR THAT FOUNDLING, OUR FALSE son, my wife and I played at parenting together, and in those early years we learned him in the ways of our family and also the first four of the elements, *dirt* and *house* and *lake* and *woods*: Cross-legged upon the fur-covered floor, we told him what we had been taught, that those four aspects were all we were—but then my wife said there was another, a fifth, and that this element was called *mother*, that it was her mothering that made the foundling, more so than any other. I thought this to be a lie but said nothing, kept silent my concern at her greedy deception—and then as I withdrew I came as well to discern elements previously unknown. Soon I wished I had spoken of these others first, to position them before her claim, or that I'd had the courage to speak of them after, to displace it: For if *mother* was an element, then so was *father*, then so was *ghost*, then so there were at least seven, a number much increased from what we had earlier believed, from what we had been told to expect, long before our arrival upon the dirt.

Over some number of months, a year, two years, we taught the foundling to crawl and then to walk, to speak in words and then in phrases. We tried to teach him how to play but failed, or else I did: At first I believed the foundling to be possessed by some strange seriousness, some unchildness, but soon I heard through a window his squeals at the tickling of his mother, at her fingers teaching him to feel ticklish.

I had never heard this laugh before, had never caused it no matter how I had thrown the boy into the air, no matter how I caught him just before he crashed, no matter what other roughhouses I taught him, as I myself had been taught.

By the time the foundling began to sing my wife's simplest songs I had learned to restrain the fingerling, but always he watched for his chances, and soon all my angers were ulcered inside me, and one by one the fingerling sought their increased company, in whatever pits they burned their slow language. My wife and I were quieter then too, gently estranged, and so from us the foundling learned to speak only slowly, a lack set against all the years the fingerling had whispered in my ear: By the time the foundling said his first word, the two matched syllables of *mother*, by then I had been convinced of my ill feelings against him.

In the months that passed he refused to learn any other word — any other but *mother, mother, mother, mother* — and at night my newly named wife held him between us in the bed, her touch always on him and never me, and at meals the fingerling conspired from my gut as my wife fussed over the foundling's every want, as their voices filled the small house, until again and again I fled the clamor of their table to go out into the moony woods, where in those days I would often find myself digging some unneeded plot, like a dog who has not yet found his bone but still wants the place to bury it.

Despite the mystery of his origins, in most ways the foundling was a boy as I had always imagined a boy would be: His learning to walk was followed by a destructive curiosity where he knocked over the carefully arranged objects of our house, cracking worse our already-bear-chipped bowls and also the wife-sung ones, or else endlessly clacking his mother's spoons against one another. Once he could better speak, he began to question every action my wife or I made, his halting sentences querying the origins of fish, the depth of the lake, the sequence of the seasons, and also crying at what he did not understand, what we could not explain into kindness, like the first time he watched me strip the hide off a deer or scrape free a fish's scales. Soon the foundling bawled every dusk when I approached the house, even when I came empty-handed: For while it was his mother who cooked for him, he saw only that it was I who fished and trapped, skinned and slaughtered and butchered, and even though he had no trouble sharing in the meals we made, it became my wife he thanked and me he feared.

I dug more holes, and because I could not dig a hole without wanting for something to put in it, for the first time I began to kill what I did not intend to use: In one hole I buried a muskrat and in another a rabbit and in another a wrench-necked goose, caught by my own hands after it squawked me away from its clutch of goslings, themselves doomed beneath my frustrated heels. My wife still maintained her garden, but in those days I also kept one of my own: For every rabbit I took from the woods, I buried two more in the clearing made when I'd cut trees for our house, so that others might grow from whence they came, and so they did grow — except that with each passing season they returned leaner and lamer, limping where they might before have hopped. It was not just the rabbits who failed, diminished by my poaching: Remember now a mink without its fur or else this beaver without the squared hatchet of its teeth, gnawing useless at a trunk it had no chance of opening. Remember this duck born with dulled beak, this peacock ill feathered to attract its mate. Remember all those other animals, blunted and endangered by my hand, and yet how could I stop, and yet what could I do except to mitigate through their bodies my most recent darkest thoughts, which always required some burial somewhere, with some thing, in some hole of my own digging.

As the foundling grew I too changed, hardened into who I would be, and soon I was burying whole deer in too-shallow holes, stepping down into their graves to snap the lengths of their antlers or else letting their branches point through the dirt, made accusing knuckles of bone. In this way all the beasts and birds of the woods gave themselves over to my traps, so that never was there a morning when I found nothing, where no fur or feather filled my gathering fists.

All the beasts and the birds, all except for one: The only animal I dared not trap was the giant bear, who I correctly feared would not suffer me to try.

Some mornings, I arrived at the burying ground to find that the bear had uncovered my plantings, had torn the flesh from off their bones so that it might eat of what I had killed but not for food—and also to bring back what it did not require. This is how I thought the bear showed me what it claimed, even unto and after death, and also what it thought of my poaching, as if I did not already know the bounds of its domain, and of all others: That the woods belonged to the bear. That the house belonged to me, or else had before, but was owned now by her, my wife. That if I wished to reduce my trespass, then the lake would perhaps be a better place in which to store my dead—if only my wife could have stomached the sight of my dragging their bodies across the dirt, of the scraped clay wounded red.

During the day, the foundling roamed often upon the dirt, sometimes in the company of his mother and sometimes alone. As he grew in size he grew braver too, but still he remained unwilling to step under even the thinnest outer trees, those still shot through with sunlight. Even with his mother at his side, holding his diminutive hands, his fingers too small for his age, even then he was afraid of everything he might have guessed lurked within those living woods, his imagination making up for his lack of experience—but could what he might have imagined be worse than the truth? Much of what happened in the woods was then my secret, and the fingerling's: the trapped and the dying beasts; the dug and filled graves; the bones thrust through the dirt, uncovered and freed to new life by the bear, then trapped and buried again.

The foundling was most afraid of the bear, that beast I had spoken of often at the table, despite the hushings of my wife, and also he was afraid of me, of the fingerling inside, that brother the foundling did not know but that I believed he sometimes heard in my voice. His fear of me disappeared only fleetingly, now and then in some lucky forgetfulness of childhood, and eventually my wife stopped bringing him near the woods, so that he would not wail at the sight of the trees, my traps, bloody me; and as they withdrew into the safety of our house I too retreated, spent more and more of my daytime on the wooded side of the tree line, that threshold's divide.

How every day I watched the foundling always choose his mother, how he preferred her lap, her end of the table, her body to curl against when dreams of the dark woods and the darker cave trembled him awake.

How his lisping voice was still better for singing than my rough and rude timbre, and how this too was a realm they shared, to which my talents granted me no entry.

How when he wanted a story, he wanted it only from her lips, and so it was her stories that formed him, never mine.

How whenever he was not with her, the foundling seemed listless, exhausted, and while she did her chores he fell asleep in odd places, tucked into a corner of the sitting room, hidden in the shaded hollows between the furniture; or upon a pile of dirty furs, ready for the washing; or in the dark slimness of the space under the bed, where I would find him snoring so slowly, balled up, legs tucked below his belly, hands folded beneath his face; and if I tried to shake him awake he would not stir, not until my wife returned to lull him from his sleep with a song or a soft word.

How the eighth element she taught the foundling was called *moon*, but when the time came my wife pronounced it *moons*, as if hers was no copy but rather some proper and equal addition to what had come before, that original to whose workings we were not then or ever privy.

How, like his mother, the foundling preferred the meat of the woods to the fish of the lake, so that always I ate alone, even when we ate together.

How even if we had not been so slowly separating, even then the fingerling would have kept us sometimes apart, his threats against the foundling enough to double my own reluctance, my own inability to father.

How I told myself I held back for the boy's safety, but how that was not the whole of the truth or even the most of it.

How by the time the foundling was with us several years — by the time the fingerling had floated within me nearly double that span—how by then I could admit the root of the fracture on our family, of the distance between my wife and I, between me and her son: Despite all my long wants, I had never thought rightly of how to be a parent or a husband, only of possessing a child, of owning a wife.

MEMORY AS NEW APPETITE, AS hunger and harriment: To wish to try to join my family in its diet, but, because I would not take back my public objections, to do so always in secret, eating only the parts of animals never eaten before, parts my wife and the foundling would not miss.

To trim the sinew from around the vertebrae of a raccoon, to gnaw a woodchuck's knuckle, to save the ears of a hare in the back pocket of my trousers.

To crack open heavy nuts taken from the cheek of a squirrel, trapped while storing its winter stock.

To throw away the stringy flesh of groundbird after groundbird, keeping only loused mouthfuls of feathers to swallow later.

To do everything differently because what was already accomplished had failed to provide what life I wished, and only some new way seemed likely to save our family from this long fall, this world beneath the slow-sinking moon, this home where there was only husband and wife and fingerling and foundling in the house, only the bear in the woods and whatever-was-not-a-bear in the lake, of which I have barely yet spoke: We knew by then the ninth element was called *bear*, and for a time nine was enough. The tenth element was in those years only intuited, and what it was best named I did not know, whether *whale* or else *squid*, else *kraken*, else *hafgufa* or *lyngbakr*; a monster to match a monster, to oppose the other merely by its existence opposite the woods, in the lake on the other side of this border of dirt, the thin territory upon which we had staked our tiny claim.

Only rarely did I have some chance to speak with my wife alone, in the language of adults, that diction now kept reserved for special occasions, rarer privacies. Always the foundling was with us, or rather with her, caught up in her skirts or tasting from her cooking spoon or toppling over in the dirt of the yard, nearby where she hung up her laundry or beat the dried mud from off our rugs, and anyway everywhere within those first rooms was within earshot of everywhere else. Now there was nowhere we could go to be together, a couple only, and now every room seemed too small, the walls close by design but made closer by the dark furs that decorated every surface.

In hopes of catching my wife alone I began to take opportunities to exhaust the foundling, to chase him around the house and the yard behind, each time inventing some game for us to share — and I remember once I made my body as big as I could, hunching my shoulders like the bear, grunting and growling my worst feelings, and the boy ran before me, stumbling and mock terrified and calling for his mother, who did not laugh at our play but at least did nothing to stop it, only folded her laundry and kept her silence. And when the foundling at last collapsed napping in the grass, then his mother carried him into the house before returning to the yard, where her wash waited unfinished, and where I waited for her.

The play had tired me too, but it had not weakened my anger, and as always when I was in my worst moods I pressed my wife to explain our son's origins, said to her, Tell me again of his conception, of the trials of your pregnancy, of threatening me with your moon that still hangs overhead.

My wife loosened one of my shirts from our line, folded its sleeves against its seams, folded it in half again, and placed it within her basket, a basket she had made. The shirt was cotton and not fur, but we raised no such crops, and so this too was sung into its shape, not trapped and skinned and sewn. All the most useful objects in our house were of her making, and what I asked her was whether the boy wasn't the same, another construct, all hers.

She was still beautiful then, her skin glossed with sun and too much moon, her eyes tired but happier than they had been in the years of our failures, and as I complained she reassured me again, said, I have given you what you wanted, or close enough.

She said, I know how many children you wanted and I know this is just one child, but you could choose to decide he was enough, to believe that one child with me was still a miracle.

She said, You are unhappy but why, when this life is almost exactly the life you wanted, that you wanted and that I agreed to give you.

But still I was unsatisfied, still I claimed that the son she had given me was not the son we had made and that somehow she had replaced him with this other, this foundling. Against these claims my wife offered no new defense, would only reassure me again, telling me not to worry, that of course he was my son, that despite the wonders of her voice her songs could not make a life. She said this again and again, against my many multiplying queries, each voiced as I trailed her around the house, following her from chore to chore, until after so many denials she changed her tack, asked quietly, What is a life lived but an array of objects, gathered or else made into being, tumored inside the wall-skin of our still-growing house? What else to make a biography of, if not the contents of these rooms?

As much as I had tried to ignore its progress, still it was obvious that the house was growing, that it grew most when I was not looking, when I was not there to catch it, and that my wife had begun to fill its new rooms with objects of her own devising, made for her own needs, those of her foundling. And then one day I returned home to find my wife not in the rocking chair where I left her, nursing her stunted son, but rather in some new room dozens of yards farther down the hallway, the hall that before went only to our bedroom but now extended past that first door, past several others I did not know. There I found them, together in a space bare of furnishings except for some bed, and there mother and son slumbered, his head laid to her collarbone, perhaps naked beneath white sheets, bodies as close as hers and mine once were.

Everything remained unsaid, our lives a stasis of secrets, and when the foundling came to me on his own then too I reached out with my hands to maintain our safest distance, pushed his outstretched arms back down to his sides, corrected his advances: When he tried to kiss me goodnight like he did my wife, I turned my stubbled cheek against his milk-stunk lips, and he was not yet strong enough to turn it back, not even with his fingers twisted tight into the scrub of my then-new beard.

The fingerling rejoiced with turns and twists through the short circuit of my guts, where he continued to make his most frequent habitation, exiting the long throw of my stomach and intestines only occasionally for the passages and pouches of lungs or liver or bladder. As yet I had not felt him within the confines of my skull-space, but often he crawled along the surface of my face, stretching my skin so that I was sure my wife might see him sliding across my features, as I thought her foundling sometimes saw. If she did, she said nothing, and eventually I came to believe that she must not. But whether her not seeing was a failure to understand or a failure to look, I did not yet want to know.

Memory as flicker, as fury: To be able to be jealous of a child was to imagine thoughts for the child that he was not yet old enough to have.

To be suspicious of our house was to be sure that in the morning there was no second floor below our cellar, and no stairs leading farther down and in, and yet in the afternoon to find both those constructions.

To have built this house without understanding or imagining that when I stopped building it would grow still—and when I was not looking, then again my wife remade what I had made, sang her own house within my house—for how else to account for all those rooms, all those hallways? How else to account for these stairs, these doors, and behind them chambers furnished with new shapes?

My wife withdrew the foundling farther from my gaze, and afterward I saw them only rarely outside the house and never far from it. I had rowed them out onto the lake, had tried to teach the foundling my habits, but those days too were ended, and again I would be the only one of my kind, denied my lineage. Now my wife and the foundling emerged from the new chambers of the house only at specific times, only at meals or else not even then, and afterward my wife retreated not by heading out of the house but by heading in, by climbing back or else down. Soon all our closets gave access to such stairs, and at the bottom of these staircases were only more doors, more halls, more rooms that for a long time stayed empty, until my wife began to fill them with the song of her voice, and after they were filled she sometimes locked their contents away, which in those days were not yet meant for me.

On the first floor, the doors were not locked as the deep ones were, and so I wandered past them in the early mornings, the late nights, the hours when my wife and the foundling slept in our shared bed or else their other bed to which I was never invited, set in a chamber I could not enter, its door suddenly barred by a mechanism I could not discover. I searched every open room, and in each one I found some newly aggressive mundanity, some object or set of wife-sung objects, their shapes familiar but their purpose inscrutable to my reckoning.

What was I to make of these rooms, the few I saw before they were shut away, and also of what they were filled with? Some held objects obvious in purposed pairings — the crib and the cradle, the bottle and the blanket — but others less so: In one room, I saw the death of a cougar but not the cougar itself; in another, the moltings of a thousand butterflies; and then a single giant specimen of the same species, bigger than any I'd seen, first flapping slowly about the room, then becoming more and more agitated as it failed to find its escape, thrashing its iridescent body against the walls of its cell until its magnificent wings were broken.

The creation of these new rooms — this *deep house* — took some toll on my wife, or else the strain of mothering the foundling began to diminish her, or else it was only the years, the first decade of our marriage already ended: Her porcelain skin paled further, shrank tight against her bones, and her long black hair shone less and less, until at last she took a pair of scissors to it, cut its length up and around her ears, and afterward it seemed her face was different than I remembered, as if her hair's framing was enough to make her one person, its absence another. Some days her voice was so hoarse from her singing that she claimed she could not speak at dinner, and at other meals she did not speak but gave no reason.

THE DAYS WERE THIEVES, AND the happier ones the worst, their distractions allowing the hours to pass unnoticed, allowing the minutes to be snatched away without knowledge of their passing. As my wife contented herself with the foundling, so I tried to make my trapping and fishing count for something, so I tried to convince myself that the fingerling could be a son all my own, son enough, and better for his embedded residency, a station where neither of us might ever lack the other, as the foundling lacked his mother at every moment: For what breast was brought soon enough after the hunger, what calming touch brought comfort in the instant of its need? No, whenever we were satisfied, then we were deluded, and in our delusions the days took from us what was ours, as wood hollowed with termites, as all iron rusted, as our clothes faded and split their machined threads, and as the home-sewn furs that replaced them grew stale and stiff. Seasons went by, each less distinct than the one before, and what world we had grew only sparser, colder: Now there was less to trap in the woods, less to catch in the lake, and what restockings there were made things only worse, as with the blunter animals the bear brought back.

And the bear? It too worsened with the days, so that everywhere I went in the woods I found its fallen fur, the marks where it scraped it free of its itching skin, against boulder and branch and now bark-bare trunk.

My wife and I, we *aged*, and although I knew it was not correct, still it often appeared our children were the agents of our diminishment: the fingerling, devouring me from within, and the foundling, always at his mother's side, taking of her body, her energy, her time, her grace. And so the days passed, and as they passed they took: Our hair grayed, our teeth yellowed, our bodies stooped across our bones, and in the mirror there was no one I recognized, only my fatter face, my beard atop that fat, my body bigger, and yet every year there was even less of me to love, to be loved by.

AND ALSO WHAT DID NOT change: Still I was only a fisherman, only a mere trapper of beast and bird, only a husband and perhaps a father—except that despite my wife's assurances I still did not believe the child I had raised with my wife was any son of mine. By the occasion of the foundling's sixth birthday, whatever my wife had done to make the child her own had exhausted my patience, and on that day I determined I would avoid its truth no more, and if she persisted in her claims, then she would cease to be even the slim wife she had become.

But how to force the issue, to put my family to the test?

As my wife had invented, so I invented too, for in that absence of rules it was often possible to make my own.

At the fingerling's suggestion, I extracted from our traps two rabbits, and from the lake I took three fish—the better, he said, to test the loyalties of our bodies against the histories of the same, to show what came from where and where each now stood. I brought my catch to her kitchen, secured it in the icebox for the making of the foundling's birthday celebration, that last shared meal, wife-cooked later that day: The smell of seared fish. The blood-and-boiling-tomatoes stink of stewed rabbit. A birthday feast made only of flesh, and no cake for baby either.

Six years old, and still the most taste he had for sweets came from the breast of her, his mother, whom he would not quit in full.

Throughout my wife's kitchenry, the foundling clutched about her aprons, her skirt hems, and likewise I clenched my left hand around my fork, my right around my knife, and also my stomach closed around the fingerling. My wife set the table, set pot and pan upon its wood, and then with our heads bowed we said our rote thanks to *woods* and *lake* and *dirt* and *house*, for the food we were about to eat, for what bounties the elements had given us. Afterward, my wife smiled or faked a smile in my direction, trying to mollify what hurt feelings I would not hide, and then she gave me the three fish she pretended I was hungry enough to eat, and to her giving I said or heard myself say No, and then, in the same voice, NO. ONE FISH FOR ME. ONE FISH FOR YOU. ONE FISH FOR THE BOY. OR ELSE WE ARE NO FAMILY.

Those were the words that I spoke to her, from behind the thickness of my beard, that newer face my wife said she did not like as much.

Those were the words she ignored as she reached for her ladle, as she scooped two steaming bowls of stew, one for her and one for the foundling, as she set his in front of his hungry fork.

I felt my words thicken the air between us, and when I stood my movements were each heavied with their vicious, viscous weight. Each move was perhaps easy to watch but harder to stop, and so even though my wife recognized my intentions, even though she shouted, rounding the room as I rose, still my hands set to gripping the edge of the table, lifting and lifting and lifting that surface until every once-right thing slid free: My ceramic plate scraped down across the up-angling wood until it hit the edge between two planks, and then the plate flipped past the foundling, who continued to sit in his chair, shock spreading across his face but too slow for safety. His utensils were still in his hands, some chunk of rabbit still skewered on the tines of his fork, and from his face his birthday expression disappeared — its happiness never a gift, only the promise of gifts — his mouth twisting as his bowl toppled into his lap, and when he at last leaped from his seat to cry out and swipe at his trousers, he took his attention off the still-climbing table, away from our last shared pot, the slipping cast-iron container, its metal barrel black and rough and alive with heat, its contents barely cooler than a boil.

I would have said I meant only to make my anger known — but then the table reared up over the foundling, and the pot struck him with a weight unexpected, its contents erupting as he crumpled, the gravy slicking his face and skin, steaming where it stuck.

How the foundling cried then! How he wailed for his mother, how he thrashed upon the floor even after my wife reached him, and how she cursed my name then, as she tore at his clothing, the furs and made cloth trapping stew against skin, as she wiped the burning food from his quick-blistered face, his tangled hair, his red-pocked arm.

As my wife lifted her naked son into her arms she said that she hated me, that I had made her hate me, and as she told me how she hated I realized I still held the table slanted, and as she told me she was leaving I lowered it back to level, let its legs thunk against the floorboards. Of all the many elements we had claimed and named, I had not given a number to *family*, had not even counted it among them, and this omission had not gone unnoticed by the fingerling, that relentless cataloguer of all my faults: Now it was *family* that would be missing, that in that moment was already gone, as my wife stood to carry the aggrieved foundling away.

I sat down on the floor of that room, the foundling's wet clothes flung everywhere, my own now drowned in a lake of stew, filthy with the smatter of vegetables ground beneath my wife's shoes, my muddy boots. Outside the windows, the sun set, but the light did not diminish: On the night of the foundling's birthday there was moon in every window, wide streamers of moonlight illuminating every surface, filling every puddle with glow. I could not stand that steaming silence so brightly illuminated, so I instead wandered down the hall to our bedchamber, tracking foul footprints to where the foundling sat on the edge of our first bed, crying from out his scorched features. I stood in the doorway and watched as my wife bandaged him shut with strips of fabric torn from the hem of her dress, swaddling his face and hands and chest to protect his open-fleshed wounds, and throughout her ministrations he would not cease his crying. She put cold compresses upon the uninjured parts of his body to cool the worse-hurt rest, but when his body could not shed the heat of his burns she did not hesitate, as always I would have hesitated. As I watched, she lifted her boy into her arms, his body limp against hers, arms and legs dangling from her grip, and then she pushed past me, out of the bedchambers and down the hallway, past the first kitchen and the first sitting room and the first nursery, that room he had so rarely slept inside, and then farther on, into the hallways beyond the one I had built, where there were more hallways still, all carved out of the dirt and into the coolness of the earth.

And what then? What words did my wife say in those last moments before their departure?

Only some song of silence: As the foundling screamed his

goodbyes, my wife relied instead on the angry quiet of her body, and as she walked away, I listened to the slimness of her shoulders, the topography of her spine, the sight of her thudding blood flushed from beneath her skinny bones, those sharp ribs pressed against her thread-worn and hem-ripped dress. What she said was nothing she could not say without her mouth closed and her eyes long-darked, already turned away — words without sound, without song — and then without further glance or gaze she was gone from my sight, and afterward the flashed shape of her absence burned hot in my eyes, and around it her silence continued speaking for years and years, remained always the sound of her saying nothing, and then the sound of the nothing said.

MEMORY AS MONTHS ALONE: TO live in a world changed by my wife but that did not contain her. In those days I began to miss her differently than I had missed her in the years we shared these rooms with the foundling, and also I came to resent the attitudes of the fingerling, who swam sharp circles around my heart and lungs, rejoicing at my wife's abandonment, her escape, that easy proof of what unsteady structure our family had been. Sometimes he choked himself into my throat, and it was in those minutes that he held court, that he showed how well he could speak in my voice, if I did not try too hard to resist.

With my mouth, the fingerling said, NOW YOU MUST GO INTO THE DEEP HOUSE.

ROUT YOUR WIFE, he said. LAY WASTE TO MY BROTHER.

CLEAR THIS DIRT OF ALL OTHER CHILDREN, he said, SO THAT I MIGHT BE REVEALED IN THEIR PLACE, SO THAT MY MOTHER MIGHT LOVE ME IN THEIR STEAD.

The fingerling, he said nothing of this to me until it was too late, and then when he did speak he said too much, on and on until I silenced him too, until I stopped his speech with an application of my fists to my stomach or throat, where I sometimes caught his shape beneath my blows, but most often I bruised only myself, marked yellow and blue guesses of where he might have been. It would be some hours before he regained his voice, but then he again spoke clear and calm and sure, uninjured behind my battered skin, and I believed what he said to me was true: My wife would not be coming back from the new house she had sung, that deep house dug below, and as long as she remained away the foundling was not coming back either.

My wife's moon loomed lower than it had before, its wider hue continuing its shift from yellow-white to pinkish-red, and as it bent the sky it also bent our seasons, so that our short fall preceded an endless dry winter, all gray skies and no snow, no rain. The woods were evergreen and so mostly kept their boughs, but even there some stands of trees lost their needles, then their cover of bark, then some thickness of their trunks, until, hollowed out, they crashed down beneath heavier winds.

In the cold those trees rotted slowly if at all, and one day I realized that the sun no longer rose as regularly as it had but rather kept its course just beneath the edge of the earth, as if it were ever almost-night or barely-morning, and only rarely after did we see its shape arcing overhead, although some measure of its gleam still curved near the horizon, glowed us long dawns, stretched days of dusk.

I continued to trap from the woods, but because I did not eat the meat my trapping created only more digging in the burying ground. I fished until the sunless air grew too cold to venture onto the water as often as I had, and on the coldest days I rested upon the dock and wondered what would happen to my fish, to whatever creature lived below the fish, the bear that was not a bear—but then the salted water did not freeze. The rest of my hours I spent in the house itself, walking not just the ground floor but also warily venturing into the first story of the deep house below, where sometimes I called my wife's name, or else the foundling's, and sometimes I did not. As I walked, gas-lamp in hand, the fingerling chattered away, often tinny in my ears, or else he spoke from lower in my body, and from both stations he urged me again to follow my wife downward, to find which of the many rooms and chambers she had entered.

I listened to his urgings, but I was not yet ready, hesitated even after we discovered the secret to my wife's doors, a banality unsuspected: All were locked with the same lock, the same set of tumblers as the house's first door, the one that led out onto the porch and the dirt, whose key I wore slung around my neck, as I had always worn it. And so none would refuse my passage, should I choose to enter.

And then one morning I found outside our front door the footprint of the bear, and more of its signs beside: its fallen fur, its spoor. Like all the other animals of the woods, the bear had never before left its shaded domain to walk exposed upon the dirt, and so beside those footprints there shivered around me my own goosed flesh, my prickled hair—for now something had lured it from its woods, and what else was there, what else had changed but the absence of my family, and then I knew that whatever pact the bear and I had enjoyed through the long years of my poaching, that unspoken truce was at last broken.

THE NEXT MORNING I SEWED for myself an armor of furs, a grotesquerie of layers upon layers, of thick skin and rough-nubbled hide, each swath stitched with a crudeness borne of my own fat fingers. I threaded together what we had meant for covering our floors and our walls and our bed, and when I was finished I draped myself tip to toe, then sewed my shape inside, made myself horrible, a beast meant to match the bear. My movements stiffened, thickened, I knelt before our hearth, wetted my fingers, dragged their tips through the cold ashes stilled there, then painted my face with what char stuck to those narrow bones, so that all that showed from within the fur was dark, cheeks and nostrils and ears and lips. Heaving beneath my burden, I tucked my skinning blade into its sheath, its sheath into the belt strained around my waist, and then I walked out the door, off the porch, around the house and into the garden, where sat my waiting traps, each wanting again for the woods.

I put my hands into that pile, and when I saw my hands next they held the only weapon I had ever understood, the only one I had ever wielded against another: not spear or axe, not machete, not bow or sling. Instead, my hands had sought what they knew, and remembered into their grip the largest of my traps, like the others in everything but size, and never before used: on this end a steel jaw, ready to be pried open, set to collapse, and on the other a chain waiting to be wrapped around my wrist and forearm, then sewn deep into the fur of my armor—and then, at the fingerling's suggestion, stitched deeper, into the arm below, so that no blow might rip it free.

Memory as reminder that I was no hunter, no good tracker: Like a fool, I first marched to the cave, but the bear did not so easily give itself up, and once inside I could not even find the tricky entrance to the lower passages where I assumed it slept.

There was only one method I had employed to cause the bear to appear, and so wearing my thick-layered suit I set my traps again, manipulated their intricate devices to capture what best beasts the woods had left, the widest-antlered bucks, never before caught and as yet undiminished, but soon broken-boned, velvet-robbed; and then another such prize, a well-plumed peacock, whose blooded coverts I twisted free from their roots, weaving their long-quilled eyes through the seams of my armor. For weeks I wore my armor and I stalked the woods and I killed every mink and otter and polecat, bashing their heads where they were caught, lifting the sewn-in trap above my shoulders, crashing it down upon their hissing, their mewing mouths. All these and more I interred beneath the burying ground, my aggression escalated so that I might fill the boneyard dirt with the best dead, so that the bear might be compelled to call them free, their shapes necessary to restock its domain. And all this time I remained stuck within my armor and then stuck to it, its threaded seams and hems leaving no place for me to slip free. For some stretch

I ate and slept and pissed and shat within, filled those furs with sweat and filth, staying in the woods until my ash-streaked cheeks were smeared with my frustration and with my disgust at my stink, and surely in this state there could have been no sneaking up on the bear, who even from within the deepest depths of its cave might have smelled my stiff-legged approach, the bloodied, muddied layers of my furs.

The woods, never loud, hushed now at my actions, until at last I woke to a morning where all my traps waited empty and quiet, there being nothing to catch or else nothing so dumb as to approach the bloody steel, the sure paths of stench and sign I left everywhere. Satisfied, I returned to the house once more, to cover myself again in hearth ash, and to wait for nightfall, the better dark within which I hoped to hunt the bear.

FIRST THE WHITE MOON RISING, then the newly red one, both wrongly full night after night and that night too, when beneath their rays I lifted my stiff-stitched and stinking self from off our porch, felt the pull of the trap's chain upon my skin, and with my loudest voice I called the fingerling to duty.

Soon I arrived at the burying ground to find the floor of that clearing flipped at last, some buried bodies of beavers and badgers and wolverines dug free of their shallow plots, their gore dried or else drying. Everywhere there was the fresh mark of the bear, its footprints wide as my face, urine like acid prickling my nostrils, fallen fur crawling with fistfuls of lice — and at that sight the fingerling squirmed nervous at the back of my mouth. I pressed him back down, and also myself forward, toward the median of that boneyard, toward what meeting awaited me there: the bear rising, unfolding its limbs from their rest, all its massive size matted in the butchery of my trappings.

The fearsome beast of our first meeting was long gone, and instead there was only this new creature, lowed, submissive in posture if not in fact, its previous wound expanded, expounded upon: The bear that stood before me now stomped unsteadily on its meat-thin limbs, its fur-torn, bone-sprung body led wobblingly forward by its squared head, that skull burst through the tearing skin of face and snout. Orbital bone gleamed bright around the jaundiced eyes it was meant to protect, those spheres drooped upon distressed tendon, sleepy on frayed muscle, and my eyes roved mad too, took in all its shape, its stomping stance, its claws flexing free of its threatening paw. Its voice tore from its lungs, the sound of that roar so fierce it stumbled me even before the bear tensed its body forward, ready to lean into the angry first step of its charge—and as it roared again I heard its true voice for the first time, a speech like no other.

Despite this show of confidence, I reckoned well the seeming diminishment of the approaching bear, for hidden inside my own hackle of found fur was the same wearied lack, the same bones carved only brave enough—and then all that remained of me arrived at its test, the bear falling upon me, all hot breath and battle, and now memory again, of conflict reached:

To plan to close the distance between us by striking the first blow.

To drop the trap from my right hand, to catch its falling chain and swing it back overhead with my left.

To watch the heavy trap orbit once, then again, the only revolutions I had the strength for, all the bear's charge allowed.

To throw my hand forward, the trap escaping my grip to slam its open sharpness into the side of the bear's opening face, catching its growl between those quick-closing jaws of my own.

To set my feet, to dig the hard heels of my boots into the dirt— the dirt beneath the woods' thin floor—and then, as the caught bear tried to wheel away, to begin to pull its face down to my level, to the dirt, turning the chain hand over hand, tightening it in my grip, wrapping its length around my forearm.

To hear the fingerling cry out as I dragged the bear, to feel his cheer loosen him from his hard small place, celebrating a victory yet unearned; and in that move he unbound what part of my resolve he had made, even as the bear turned back, as it charged again, as even with my trap undoing its face it closed our slim distance, intending to undo much more of me.

The bear roared, its voice constrained but never caught, and then it stood into that sound, lifting the enormous dark of its body upon its hind legs, and me with it, up from off my own thinner limbs. Its head was now three lengths above the forest floor, my trap still embedded in the crushed flesh and scraped bone of its cheek, and from the other end of the trap's chain I was left to dangle and kick and also to support my sewn-in arm with the other, trying to reduce the pull of that deadly weight, its tearing free.

My armor came apart beneath every swipe of the bear's claws, its uselessness made more obvious with each tugging of the bear's trapped head, each new blow ribboning my flesh beneath. Before long my caught shoulder separated from its socket, muscle and bone pop-popping beneath my skin, and now both the bear and I were howling, our shared frustration loud enough to empty the woods, to drive every still-living thing from that burying ground.

The bear continued to stand, swung and batted and pulled against my caught chain until it damaged not just my body but its own. Inch by inch I fell, my weight dragging the trap down the bear's muzzle, that sliding steel unbinding some rare part of its still-skinned skull, squeaking metal on bone, scratching a swath of hair from off its face as it worked itself free. My feet kicked for the relief of the ground, but despite my slow falling, the last few inches remained a gap I couldn't yet close, and as I swung within the bear's anger, I continued to be caught by its blows, my tattered shirts filling with more and more of my dumb blood. In my shoulder I watched some strained bone at last break through the skin, and when I nearly fainted at the sight and the spilling, then the fingerling inserted himself into the action, keeping me awake, urging my eyes again, commanding me to hang on, to somehow climb the chain with my good hand even as he moved out of my chest and into my trapped shoulder. As he stretched his length up that side of my body, I felt how he worked his own secret skill, making some new connections to bridge muscle to tendon, tendon to bone, and above it all he spun skin to contain what he had repaired, and as I realized what he had done I cried out again, all at once so sore afraid.

M Y REBUILT SHOULDER HELD, AND upon its strength I pulled myself up the chain toward the bear's throat, where I thought to put my skinning blade to right use, but then came some cruder event, the fingerling snapping, or else something snapping in the fingerling, his cries echoing inside mine, their loudest sound escaping my mouth to be mistaken as some fiercer threat. The bear howled at my howls, tossing its head and its shoulders and me too, my body swinging in time with its movements until at last I fell free, the momentum of my bloody weight screeching bone, pulling the trap's jaw clear of the bear's snout, the bear's freedom and mine bought at the cost of most of its nostril, and also a ropy skein of maggoted, loused fur torn from nose to ear.

I faced the untrammeled bear, its open roaring, and what latest bear met my looking, enormous upon its hind legs: I saw for the first time its rows of sore-pocked nipples, four across its chest exposed from thinning fur, nearly choked shut by the bone sprung through the bear's winter coat, then the lower set, the pair almost hidden behind a furred thickness still untouched by the surrounding decay. The bear waited until it saw I had seen, and then it laid its length upon the forest floor, rolled its body back and forth across the madness of mud our tangle had made, as if the cool earth might soothe the damage I had done its face.

Or rather, not its face, but *hers*: She whined and whimpered in the agony of her ruined mouth, pressed it hard against the forest floor, biting and tearing at the earth, yellow teeth staining with dark dirt. How little I still knew of the bear then, despite all the other mammals I had trapped and gutted, despite all the others and parts of others I had buried, and all the dusks and dawns I had stood on the dirt side of the tree line, watching her move about the clearing of the burying ground, waiting for her to leave before I made my own approach, some leftover rabbit in my hand, and how wrong I was to believe the bear a he instead of a she —

For now I was sure the foundling was no boy but rather a cub, stolen from this once-sleeping mother, this wooded power who slept no more.

And no wonder the sun could not rise. No wonder winter could not fully come. No wonder in those days it was always the far end of fall, always almost-night, when such a thing could come true, such a thing as the theft of a cub, as a song to make a boy.

All this, because my wife took what was the bear's to love and loved it herself, because she entreated me to love it as she did.

All this, and still there was also with me my own secret child, the one we made but did not finish, whom I had not revealed, only buried away inside my breast and belly.

I stood up into that fear, into the pain that surrounded it, and on unsteady feet I spoke to the bear.

I said, I know what my wife took from you.

I said, I know you have come to my house looking for what is yours.

I said, The child you seek, I promise it has never been mine. I have not claimed what remains yours to claim, or if I have, it has only been these small beasts buried here, these trifles, of no importance to me.

But never your child, I said. Never that.

To the bear, whining, writhing beneath my words, I said, It was my wife who made your cub her own, who made him no bear at all.

As I spoke — as I waited for the bear to respond — I found I could not lift my right arm, its length still swaddled in deep-sewn chain. The impulses of my brain failed again and again to reach the nerves of that limb, and I saw how that length of my armor was swollen with what I had spilled. I began to fear I would lose the arm, until what else was there to do but make any mistake that might first save me, and still I swear I did it almost without thinking — or else it was only what thoughts floated behind my speech, the speech I spoke to the bear even as my remainder asked the fingerling for his help, asked without knowing if he could — and then the fingerling agreed, too eager, and only once my body thrummed with his process did I keen the cost of our agreement: He knitted my flesh, remade complete what he had begun while I hung from the bear's grip, but also he took some other part of me with which to do so, as his mother had done to make her moon, forming it not only from song but from some fraction dug from each of us, and for some short time after I would be less whole than before, even past what fractures I already possessed, and with each stitch that pushed the trap-chain from out my skin or reknit my flesh, so some other bound the fingerling tighter to me than ever before.

With my arm again wholed, I set my knife to quickest work, cutting through layers until I had shed my shredded armor, and then

I pulled tight the remainder of my undershirt to cover the still-flapping skin of my chest and belly. The bear's lungs sucked air and breathed blood, so that her teeth specked with the evidence of her deep wounds, but what was there to do for her within my few powers? I was not the healer my wife was, not the shaper of flesh she had somehow become. Softly I stroked the bear's coat, paining myself not to pull even more fur from her already-unthreaded skin, and then the bear roared, and with her roar she told me what mistake I had made: Until my confession, she had not known where her child went, had thought him dead, his now-furless smell so alien she had not guessed my wife's son had been that cub so long gone missing, so furiously missed.

T HE BEAR DID NOT SPEAK precisely, could not form the mouth-shapes necessary to make the words of our language. I moved to make some response to her roarings — this speech so unlike my own yet somehow translated by the fingerling — but that ghosted son moved first, marshaled his new shapes to possess some smaller set of tools, my tongue numbed as he muscled behind it his own wet weight. As he spoke he swam from my head to my heart to my many other hurts, and then to all of them at once, something he had not before been able to do, and even as I struggled to understand the bear I also feared to know the powers this new ability portended: The fingerling's securing of my shoulder — and the snapping that had followed — had done him some damage, and now he was not just one shape but many. In each of the wrong and wounded spaces within me, some fingerling came up to call a chorus, to give voice to WHAT NOW, to WHAT NEXT, to WHAT COWARD, WHAT COWARD — and how I tried to ignore him, the many of him there were, and how he expanded everywhere against my shattered nerves, so that I might not.

I followed the bear into the mouth of her cave, where my wife and I had made our temporary home, then we descended after her into the deeper tunnels, where I had searched for my wife after I first saw the bear, when my wife disappeared into the earth for some hours or days. Together we went deeper still, but always along the main path, ignoring the branching side halls and rubbled chambers I saw spiraling away into the dark. In that structure there were no doors, only loose pilings of stones, and through their impermanent barriers I did spy some snatch of what lay there, stolen away: Here one of my traps, there a ripped and discarded skirt my wife had thought well lost.

Soon we arrived in the chamber where I assumed the bear had hibernated, where presumably she had been asleep when we first came to the dirt to build our house — or at least that theory accounted for the long habitation evident in that chamber, with its layers of bedding, of bent and torn bones, near fossils. Here too there were some scraps of fabric, ripped shreds of paper that might have belonged to us, or anyone else like us, and everything in that chamber smelled of the bear — urine and rot and feces, dank and fetid, damp fur and dug dirt and stalest milk — and while I continued to be curious about what I had found, I did not have much longer to look.

The bear placed before me some small bundle of furs, and I needed no imagination to recognize their origins. She unfolded them with her paws, opened them below my slumped body, and then after she retreated I knelt in the space she allowed and gathered the furs into my arms: Here was snout and claws attached to more fur, thick fur lined underneath with fat, all somehow still fresh, ready again to be the makings of a better-made bear than the one before me. The linger of my wife's perfume remained, proof enough that it was indeed my wife who had song-skinned the bear's cub, and while the bear watched, I rubbed my fingers down the seams of her cub's separation, feeling for the places where he had ceased to be a bear, a connection severed as he became a boy, birthed out of this child already alive, already once made flesh from flesh.

The bear roared and then roared again, and in this roar I saw her cave before we came to it: How deep beneath the woods the bear slumbered then, and within her the cub, some drifting egg, some fertilized idea, unplanted.

And in this roar, more worries, that if she was disturbed before her cub was born, then he might not be born at all, or might be born in the wrong place, where he would not survive; that if the coming of her cub did not cause her to stir, then there would be a time when the cub was awake and alone in the cave, vulnerable.

And in this roar, why she put her den so low, why the entrance of her cave was so complicated, the tunnels deeper so distracting, dazing enough that some simpler thief might have lost her way, might have sought instead some easier prize to steal — but not my stubborn wife, not this mother capable only of ghosts, who would one day want more than anything a baby of her own, a baby she might give to me.

And in this roar, how after we came my wife crept downward through the bear's tunnels, filling her boredom and loneliness with exploration, while on the dirt I toiled with my hands to raise us our house.

And in this roar, how my wife first found the bear, long asleep, long pregnant as my wife would one day wish to be pregnant.

And in this roar, how my wife had placed her hands upon the

bear's swelled season, her stomach still full-furred in those days, and how my wife had held her hands there until she felt the four-footed kick of the cub.

And in this roar, what happened next, the first split of the bear's own fur, the first growth of bone or shell to cut its way out, wounds made by my wife's songs, by their desperate and varied attempts to slow the bear, to speed my wife's escape after she was caught.

And in this roar, the too-early labor of the bear caused by the same, her cub loosened by the bear's chase of my wife, by her premature return to the woods, to the tree line where I saw her for the first time.

And in this roar, how the bear tried to return to sleep, to slow the cub's coming, how in her dreams she believed it a thing done, and yet how as she slept the cub did come.

But first how her strange pregnancy seemed to take *years*, the bear thought or else dreamed, and still the cub was born too soon after the bear's angry pain, her destruction of our cargo, her retreat into the depths: her cub then a tiny thing, unable to care for himself, but with a dozing mother too hurt to nurse him right, unable to do anything but sometimes sing some simplistic bear-song, a lullaby meant to slow his growth until the bear could be made right, well healed enough to mother him.

How one day when the bear awoke, her slowed cub was gone, and she did not know where he had gone.

And then this last roar, all the truth left to tell: The bear told me that the father of her child was a bear. She told me that the father of her child was not a bear. She told me that the father of her child was here. She told me the father was not here. She told me that the father of her child was nowhere, and also everywhere, as long as everywhere did not extend to the other side of the lake, the other side of the mountains, that rich earth where things were less simple than they were upon the dirt or within the woods or beneath the lake, and so perhaps there was even more that was possible, more than she remembered.

Perhaps, she roared or, rather, not the word but what words I heard in the sound: Perhaps, but even if that was so then still that was not the way here. And in her voice I heard something so like the voice of my wife, some similar tone to that with which she had told me how we would make the dirt our own, how with new rules we would shape from it the world we wanted.

The bear woke me from my memories with more of her voice, and then she told me that upon the dirt between the lake and the woods, always there were two that appeared, and always the two made a single child.

She told me that now there were four, and too many children besides, because ours was both boy and cub, and perhaps none of the four was set upon the right place, nothing shaped as it should be shaped, and when she was done telling me this she told me what she thought should be done to put our world to right—what should be done to my wife and to one other—so there might be a right number of each, of male and female, mother and father, parent and child.

With loud and quiet roars, with a variety of vocalizations I had never heard before, a bear-song simpler than our own speech but supple enough for possible truth, she told me that if I would return her cub to her—and if I would also punish my wife for taking him—then she would take care of the other, my own complement I had not yet met, and afterward the numbers would be better balanced, as always they had been intended.

I nodded as I listened, but I knew she was not quite right, for in all her calculations she did not count the fingerling. He was my secret alone, and so long as he was within me, then there was no proper math.

THE BEAR'S CARAPACE SHIVERED, HEAVED. She lowered her shoulders to the ground, then motioned with the wedge of her head that I might climb up. I searched for purchase among her bones, dug out handfuls of fur and slipped flesh before finding promontories on which to make my nervous clenching, and after I was right-straddled atop her the bear leaped out of her chamber, climbing sure and swift into and up and through the deep tunnels to the surface. Outside her cave, the bear charged through the woods, whipped through branch and thorny bramble until my face and arms were scratched and scraped, each new blemish drawing what blood remained, and before I could voice any complaint we were arriving, already back at the burying ground.

There the bear slowed, circled once, then stopped and stood upon her hind legs, raising her half-furred face above her shoulders so that as she ascended I fell from her back, landed hard. Freed of her burden, she remained standing to howl at the moons, which at first continued their slow arc unfazed by what sound she hurled at their shapes, no matter how she carried on.

Frustrated, the bear lowered herself, then stood to howl once more, and this time I thought I saw my wife's moon shake in its circuit.

And so again I said that I would do as I had been asked, this time in my own voice: I would enter the house, I would seek out my wife, and in the deepness I would convince her to give up the foundling.

OR ELSE TAKE HIM FROM HER, said the fingerling, from out of my mouth, and then again the bear shook its hackles, again it roared until all the woods and my wife's moon shook around us, and still there came more sound from the bear, more spit-flecked thunder and command, and then from the surrounding graves came that exodus I knew nightly happened but which I had never before seen. As I watched, broken-boned deer and elk and moose pushed forth from the forest floor, and then cougars and muskrat, wolves and coyotes, beavers and squirrels and rabbits and skunks and chipmunks and wild goats and boars, partridge and pheasant and peacock and grouse and all other manners of beast and bird, each called by the bear from whatever shallow place I had buried its shell. I recoiled as they stumble-rushed into the thickets or failed to take flight, for all the wrongs I had done now came past me on all sides, their injuries grotesque, and yet how I would commit the same wrongs again, how I knew I would: The wants that had prompted me to break their bones and beaks, to rip their fur and feathers, to taste their oddest parts, none were resolved, and when I was remade I too might be less than I was.

The bear knocked me flat with the heavy paddle of her paw, then held me against the soft-flipped dirt: With tooth and claw she undressed me until I was naked and then again until I was stripped of my nakedness. My wounds oozed, fed the roots below, and when I was empty of blood I took one more breath and then I was empty of that too, and as I suffered, the bear breathed herself into my unskinned body, filling me with her coughs and her wheezes and also her musk, her wild smell which ever after leaked from my pores.

Within the bear's heated speech, I heard her melody, like that of my wife's but simpler, without proper words, and with that sound the bear scabbed each wound, filled each divot with song-made flesh, as my wife might have done to make her foundling. This new body, it was meant to last the long journey ahead, that departing beneath the dirt to which we had agreed, and with its completion the fingerling grew excited from his many perches—and in that moment I became something else, other than what I had been—some not-quite-husband, a dream of the bear, as the bear was perhaps the dream of the woods, of the cave beneath, set in motion toward what she wanted most, toward what I or the fingerling had agreed, a pact without which she would not have rebuilt this body upon my bones: I would enter the deep house, and there I would find my wife and convince her to give up the foundling and also to again skin him as a bear using his right and previous fur, which I would carry with me into the earth. In return we would not be punished for our crimes, neither me nor my wife, and so we might be free to leave the dirt, escape back around the lake, to our fathers' country over the mountains, or else to some other distant land, like this one but also better emptied.

We would be saved, the bear promised—but if my wife would not give up the foundling, then I was to take him by deception or blood, and then when I returned there would be other rewards, if I chose to remain to receive them.

For this and less I betrayed our marriage, as slim threaded as it then was, and for this I am ashamed, and yet in my defense what can I say but this: Without that betrayal, how else would I have gained the strength to descend into the deep house, to seek the reunion that could only happen within those long halls, those strange chambers slung toward the bottom of those steepest stairs, spiraling down.

B UT FIRST WINTER CONTINUED UPON the dirt, and sunless days too, and as I watched, my wife's moon dug hollow the night sky, so that what few stars existed must have lived only in the short margins of our steep-sloped horizons, starved of their long circuits, the vacuum they'd before been free to roam. All our atmosphere filled with clouds heavy with rain and snow and sleet and hail, their darkness above us, and yet it never rained or snowed or sleeted or hailed, the strained sky making nothing more than a terrible buzzing, heard whenever I looked up at its unturned arc, and for some time I did not see the bear again, but sometimes I saw her footprints, marked all over the rough dirt — and then, after she sickened further, not footprints but some new dragging, a scrape instead.

The footprints led often past the house and toward the lake, but the scrape appeared motioned in the opposite direction, wet from the water, then from the blood leaking out of the bear from the shore to the dirt to the woods. I wondered if all I had to do to save my wife was to wait for the bear to die, but the fingerling denied even this hope: NO, he said, THE BEAR'S DEATH CHANGES NOTHING, AND STILL THERE WOULD BE THE FALLING MOON.

The fingerling commanded me out of the house and down the slippery glass of the path to the lake, following the scrape to the salted shores of our beach, where we came upon some enormous mass the likes of which I had never imagined, all of its blubbered weight rent unrecognizable by claws and teeth some time before, then left to float, to bob up and down upon the waves until at last it had stranded there in the night, brought high onto the beach by the strange tides our two moons had wrought. What was it that so deeply hurt the bear, what was it that she had killed? For long minutes I stared, unable to make sense of what I saw. It shared no shape I already knew, was instead all shapelessness all over, made punished flesh or cracked mantle or torn appendages, and before its bloated stench all my guesses seemed wrong.

And I wondered: What were the bounds of its shapelessness?

Was it shapeless like a squid, or shapeless like a whale?

THE NEXT TIME I STEPPED across the threshold of my house I shut the door behind me, locked it tight against the dirt. The door's key swung chained from my neck, then went tucked inside my clothes, over my heart, cold among the hair and the gooseflesh. In haste, so that I might not lose my slight courage, I gathered the few provisions I thought I would need, a single satchel's worth: only some salted and smoked fish, my gas-lamp and torches and flint, a soon-useless ball of string; the skinning blade; and also what the fight with the bear had won me, the writhing cub-fur with which I was to confront my wife, which I was to guilt her into again clothing the foundling inside.

MEMORY AS FIRST EXPLORATION OF the deep house, as this progression of rooms: To follow the many staircases down to the many landings, the many hallways branching out from behind progressively heavier doors.

To open the first rooms and find the deep house made now a palace of memory, a series of rooms in which what I had forgotten had been curated, collected together with what I had tried to forget, and also with other moments that had occurred only in dreams, or else not at all, not for me.

To find in each room some unadorned spectacle, my wife or me or us together, with or without those children we had failed to have, plus the one she had stolen, that she had passed off as our own. Or not passed off, but made true: It was in those passages that I saw how even if I had not accepted the foundling into my family, still my wife had accepted him into hers, put him at its center, a space I believed I had once occupied, and so our house was divided, and then divided again and again, because what house might stand against a child loved by only one parent, when the jealous other held that same child in suspicion and contempt?

And how for me the fingerling remembered everything.

How the fingerling saw even what I would have left undiscovered, what I did not want to share with him or any other child.

How even then he rode most often in my belly, in my thigh, in my throat, so that he might always be close to the skin, soaking in the new airs I moved my body through. And so he was there too in each of those many rooms, where otherwise there would have been only me, always me, me lonely and me alone among the tiny domains of my wife, sung into being as she passed, echoed throughout the deepening dirt.

In the first room I found piled the cargo we lost to the bear: Here again were the broken vases and cracked crystal, the shattered punch bowls, the punched-out platters.

Here were the shredded rags of my wife's dress, and beside them my boutonniere, meant to be preserved inside a translucent bubble, now freed from where it had been glassed.

Here was the intricate mechanism of a handmade clock, gifted and then broken, stopped as all other clocks were eventually stopped.

All these objects, seemingly each its own but merely parts of a whole, what in the cave we had lost.

And in this room: her wedding ring, discarded. She had improved everything I had given her but not this, and so its simple band remained only what it had ever been. I held the ring in my hand, and then I took off my own ring, and I laid both upon the stones, touching. Rings had been insufficient to fasten us together, and it would take more than rings to rebind what had been broken.

AND LESS TO END IT, reminded the fingerling. AS YOU HAVE PROMISED. AS I PROMISE YOU WILL.

And in this room: the sound of my wife's knuckle first sliding beneath the beaten silver of that ring, a sound never before heard, or else forgotten amid all the other business of our wedding day.

And in this room: the footprints she made on the beach where we were wed, where we had stood atop that platform, separated by the priest and then joined by the same, and all this upon that other sunnier shore, where it was not always summer but where often it was summer enough.

And in this room: where my footprints that evening were, not always at her side, only sometimes so. And how I wished it had been different, that I had not walked away at the beginning of our marriage, when I thought it would always be so easy to return.

And in this room: the words I used nearly every summer after, to beg from her one more child, even after she was determined only to stop the trying and also before she found she wanted her motherhood again, wanted it this time for herself, wanted it more than even I had ever wanted or realized.

And in this room: the scent of my wife's perfume as she passed, a smell once lovely, now stale as glue. And how I missed its original, how I had missed it.

And in this room: every graying hair she pulled from her head or her body in the failed years between the fingerling and the foundling. Every piece of skin she rubbed raw in the bath, when between miscarriages she could not scrub away the hormone-stink of motherhood, falsely begun. All that hair and skin, stuck wet to the floor.

And in this room: A white suit that no longer fit. A shirt that wouldn't button, a tie that drew its knot too quick around the neck. The relics of a body betrayed against itself, and against my wife, who had not agreed to love what fat and hair it acquired, nor the blank spaces replacing what it had lost, those first few teeth, those other small kindnesses.

And in this room: My wife's garden, if she had not abandoned its offerings to eat the meat of the woods. What she might have grown with the labors of her hands instead of the song of her voice. What this dirt would have yielded to us, if only she had again given the sun leave to shine.

And in this room: a silver bowl full of her tomatoes, one taste of which revealed the tang of their song-stuff, their lack of right reality, despite skin, despite juice and seeds.

And in this room: all the faces of the fish I had taken from the lake, piled into a single mash of eyes and gills, teeth and scales. How surprised I was to see them, and how easy it was to forget how many lives I took just to keep myself alive, to feed my wife and the foundling. All these bodies, knifed open so we might continue another day.

And in this room: The death of a badger, cradled in steel, rehashed. The static of an action worn down by repetition, this series of moments brought to completion only to begin again, reduced, semi-badgers torn and tortured into some novel shape.

And in this room: an empty space in which, if I had watched long enough, the badger might eventually have been made separate from the trap, freed from its circumstance, if not the damage done.

And in this room: a floor of hides, stitched from the skins of what I had trapped, where I could not stop myself from kneeling upon the floor, from digging the hooks of my fingers into its stitching. I pulled and pulled and undid some of its ties, and from beneath I revealed only more flooring, more skins sewn to skins, and soon there was around me a pit of flesh, a hollow stinking of its taxidermy, and below that only more skin, only more fur.

And in this room: the buzzing of bees and then, elsewhere, another room, full of bees. Two separate rooms, one with the bees themselves, silent, and the other filled only with their sound. How many more rooms I knew there must be if that continued. How much more house it took to keep things separate, to break them down.

And in this room: the smell of decomposing onion and beet, potato and rutabaga — all that vegetal rot.

And in this room: The last sunflowers of my wife's garden, the first that stretched their petals toward her red moon instead of the sun that barely again rose over the dirt; and if the light of the moon was mere reflection, and the light of two moons doubly so, why then their different hues, against the vast black of the sky?

And in this room: a fistful of black seeds.

In the next room, the shell of the bear: her proud bones stuck through her skin, her bristled fur fallen like pine needles. Her claws pulled from their moorings, her teeth loose in her jaws, her breath rotten as fallen bark, worm-struck as the earth beneath her woods, stinking of meat eaten long past its date, dug up.

And in this room: my wife's favorite dress, worn the first time she danced with me. How when I held the fabric to my face I smelled nothing, because the smell of her sweat was in another room.

And in this room: a well-scrubbed floor, and on it a well-scoured pot, scratched by the removal of meals we shared, of meals we ate apart.

And in this room: a bowl made of mirrors, so that as I drank of it, it drank of me.

And in this room: the song of the stars, never heard after it was silenced above the dirt, and before that never this clearly. How I had forgotten even what I had forgotten, this series of notes that made a song that made a story, all so hard to retell without their sharp light present, hard to hear or hum even when the stars yet hung from the sky, and impossible now that their shapes had been extinguished. And again my wife had remembered, as I had not.

And in this room: lightning. And in this room: thunder. And in this room: how long it had been since it rained.

And in this room: the smell of a mother's sadness, but not my wife's. Hers I would have recognized easily, but this one took some longer effort, for what man could know the tears of a bear, the way her sorrow-sweat stinks, soaked through fur and hide?

How now I could, because the bear had filled my skin with her breath, and if some part of me was the fingerling, so perhaps some other portion was the bear.

And in this room: How my wife made the bear weak. How she lay flat upon the dirt, upon the dirt floor of our cellar, and put her cheek upon the ground. How she whispered songs into the earth, how with those songs' reverberations she lulled the bear to sleep even as she kept her sleep restless, to delay her rival's tracking, her waking attempts to move upon the dirt. How the wounds my wife had given the bear worsened, how the bone snapped free of the rib meat, of the fleshy parts of the neck.

A ND IN THIS ROOM, THIS new series of rooms that followed: My wife walking out of the house and across the dirt.

My wife lifting the hem of her skirt above the brambles at the tree line, choosing her steps carefully as she navigated the trapped woods.

My wife slowing to look at deer and elk, muskrat and wood-chuck, rabbit and squirrel, all still whole and hearty, sure sign this memory preceded the foundling, our finished family.

My wife stopping to smile from within a pillar of sunlight, such shafts already rare and soon to be rarer still.

My wife not carefree in that dappling, but preparing, gathering strength.

And in this room: the entrance to the cave at the center of the woods, marked only by her footprints in the muck, headed in.

And in this room: my wife traversing the many chambers of the bear's cave, all descended from the one in which we so briefly lived when first we came to the dirt.

—

And in this room: my wife gathering the yawning cub below into her arms, then putting some few furs to rest in its place.

And in this room: the bear half lidded, locking its gaze with my wife's, parent-that-was to parent-to-be. How angry the bear's yellow eyes were, and how sad my wife's.

And in this room: the song with which she beat and battered the bear.

Then another room, with the bear's own song, its curdling attempt to fight in the manner of my wife.

And then another, with the secret of my wife's ears, stopped up safe with wax and tiny balls of feathers.

And in this room: My wife holding the bear down with her song, then lulling that giant back to sleep. Then leaning in close, putting her lips inside the tickle of the bear's ear, and there whisper-singing a lie, a vision to replace the truth: to make the bear believe she had awoken already and in her hunger devoured her cub, so that it might live no more, so that it might be back inside her, a jumble of leg and paw, face and fur, all feeding the one who fed it.

And in this room: How my wife was not sure she had succeeded until months later, when the bear awoke from her long hibernation to howl her shamed horror into the earth, to fill her cave with worse sound, to shake the earth and also the trees above, frightening the birds to flight, the beasts to quivering in their burrows and their beds, and afterward the woods seemed emptier, occupied only with what ruined fauna the bear and I would make together.

And in this room: A single moment, captured during the long lonely climb out of the cave, the sleeping cub cradled to her breast. A single note of the song she sung as she climbed, that secret song I knew so well, which she had practiced upon the dirt while I slept locked inside our bedchambers.

A single note, and yet how I knew what it could do, and what other notes would follow, and how I knew that even before she emerged into the air of the woods the cub was no cub at all.

How I knew all this at that first note, knew it even before I found the other rooms containing some other single sound of that transformation from bear cub to foundling, finished even before she arrived at our front door, the entrance to a house at last filled with family.

And in this room: again a ball of furs, same as I carried in my satchel, but memory made, song grown.

How I removed the true fur, bear given, and how I held it in one hand, then this song-made copy in the other.

How when I picked the two furs up again, I could not remember which was which, and so took them both.

And in this room, in these rooms, a vision: mine or my wife's, of all the stars that had fallen out of the sky and into the lake; of those stars falling still, descending sputtering through the deepest water, then past into some other darkness, where for a time they might light the wide hollows below.

———

A ND IN THIS ROOM: THE love letters we wrote to each other in the months of our courtship, aflame. This then the last seconds of their existence, when we burned them on the eve of our wedding, when my wife said that the words inked by my hand and by hers were the words of lovers but not spouses and that after we were joined we would need new letters with which to profess new promises.

But never again did we write each other, because afterward we always had each other so close.

What I would have given to be able to stand the heat of those old immolations, to have been brave enough to thrust my hand into their flaming shapes so as to read whom it was my wife had loved, so as to again become that person.

And in this room: the moment of our first lovemaking, which did not occur in the house but in that other country where we lived when we were first married, its cities once reachable by the road that led around the lake that, until we lost the head of its trail, could have taken us back home.

And in this room: a moment even earlier, the first time my wife raised her dress to me, exposing her battered shins. And then in another the first time I saw the bruises that blacked her knees and tendered the skin of her thighs.

And then, in another, the first time, long after those first times, when I realized she'd done this to herself.

And in this room: a memory of my parents, a story I had told my wife.

My parents, who should have taught me how to be a parent myself.

Who tried but perhaps could not succeed, for what did they know of families on this side of the lake, the mountains?

In their own country, children lived and lived and lived, and so many of our structures were unnecessary there, would be bright madness if erected in their shining world.

And in this room: the blanched face of the father of my wife in the moment I asked for his daughter. How it was my wife's permission I needed, and yet I did not seek it until others had promised her hand.

And in this room: my father's voice, telling me the purpose of a marriage was the improvement of a man and a woman, each meant to make the other better.

It is enough, he said, and also, You cannot expect to make the world better, not by any love.

He said it was only to my wife that I was responsible for my actions, and only to me that she could be held to the same standards. And as he said this I knew he believed it, that he did not know he was wrong, and that in his wrongness it was his duty to me he had not considered.

And in this room: the smile on his face as he said those words, which at the time I mistook for friendship, a bond we had not previously enjoyed.

And in this room: My younger father, years earlier, telling me what it means to be a man. My ungrayed mother, telling me what it means to be a husband. These two talks, which did not take place at the same time, joined here as they never were, so that I would be reminded that their advice was anything but the same thing—and also I wondered how my wife knew, how she knew these parts of me to take, to put into her own deep house as if they were hers—and it was the fingerling who provided the answer, who reminded me of what flesh she took to make her moon.

And in this room, in this series of rooms: Why we moved to the dirt between the lake and the woods, the reason different than what always I had believed before. And how this was something she never told me, even though we were husband and wife. And in each room of that floor one action of a sequence was made distinct from the last, so that the crush of her father's body atop her mother's was separated from how his knees punched into her thighs, pinning them to their mattress. Then the blows she struck across the meat of his forearms as they moved his hands to her throat. Then how her father choked her mother. Then how he lifted her head by the throat, then how he struck the headboard with her skull until he had broken both.

And in this room: another reason my wife had not at first wanted children of her own, even as I wanted them more than anything else. The genes of a killer, the genes of someone killed; half of what her parents had, but which half?

And in this room, another space, filled by the fingerling saying, THAT IS HOW IT SHOULD BE. THAT IS HOW YOU SHOULD MAKE IT TO BE.

And in this room: How my wife had known what her father was, how he had hurt her too, and how she had lived with the hurt because it meant that her mother received less.

How after my wife left his house for mine, then her mother had no one left to protect her.

How my wife blamed herself for this, and how she also blamed me, for taking her away.

And in this room: The sound of my wife singing herself to sleep. The sound of her voice keeping her company. The sound of a song that made temporary ghosts to appear and then to sing her songs along. How she punished herself for her loss. How she promised that her own children would be born into a world without sadness, without tragedy, without death, or at least without the death of parents. How she determined to make that world and only then to give me the children I claimed to want, and how she planned to keep those children safe.

How if she could not keep this promise, she would rather not have any children at all, no matter how I begged.

And what bruises accompanied these words.

What burns and shallow cuts.

What years those wounds lasted, scabbed over, healed, replaced, scarred white.

Those pale textures, all previously hidden in places I would never look, or where I had stopped looking, or else in plain sight where again I failed to see or understand.

And in this room: how I told my wife that by taking her away I would keep her safe.

On some new dirt, I told her, she would no longer hurt herself, no longer visit upon her body what frustrations she gathered from the busy world around her, its tall buildings, its crammed streets.

Our new world, it would be quieter, simpler.

Our new world, it would be just her, would be just me, just us and the babies I then hoped — that I hoped we both hoped — would become our family.

As if to prove my love I should remove her from all that she knew. As if to keep her mine, I had to share her with no one.

And in this room: my wife saying she does not want children, that she has never wanted children.

And in this room: my wife saying that she is tired, that her body aches, that her breasts are sore from years of unpurposed lactation, and that she does not want to live this way.

And in this room: my wife saying Please, saying Please stop.

And in this room: My wife pleading that a husband and a wife are still a family. That two are enough.

And then, in another room down the hall, my voice replying, my voice saying, No.

And in this room: all the arguments by which I hoped to leverage her first to try and then to keep trying, even as in the aftermath she hurt her body, then the house and the dirt and the sky.

And in this room: How inside a mother bear a cub might float for months before starting its arc toward birth. How it might remain a tiny bundle of cells, dividing slowly, until the bear's body decided conditions were right, that there was enough food stored inside the sleeping mother, enough of whatever else it took to make a cub. How my wife thought of this often, this bear-knowledge she knew, as pregnancy after pregnancy we failed to fill her with what stuff she needed to bring forth our child, our children.

And in this room: the moment of the fingerling's conception, when the half-body of my making entered the half-body of my wife's, and how from that moment part of me grew inside part of her. And even in that moment her seeing how jealous I was, despite how I tried to hide it, from that first moment until the one months later, when the fingerling passed from her body and into my hand, where while she howled I claimed the two halves of us for myself, so that they might grow inside my flesh instead.

And in this room: the shape of that heartbreak, a slim black tear, the length of a finger.

And in this room: the fingerling's crib, its small wooden frame, its thin pad and song-spun blanket filthied with the garden dirt.

And in this room: the times my wife touched me while I was asleep, happening here in sequence but cut away from their context, their chronology recognizable only by the changes in my body, in hers. How long she persisted. How I thought throughout that we were already estranged, that in our silences we were to come undone, unravel from our bonds. And yet in this room she ran her hands beneath the sheets, across the width of my widening back, traced her fingers through the salts of the day's working, then wrapped her arm around the slumbering bulk of my belly, that round shape girthed heavier than that she had first married, that she then still loved.

And in this room: How I touched her too. How every time it left a mark.

AND IN THESE ROOMS, MORE component parts, more wife-shaped pieces of our past, and as we walked I decided that despite the fingerling's insistence and my undiminished fear of the bear I would find some way to escape the bonds of my promise. I told the fingerling I would continue to pursue my wife and the foundling but not to hurt them worse, only to beggar myself before them, to bloody my knees with my apology, and the fingerling said, NO, said, WE GO NOT TO FIX THAT FAMILY BUT TO END IT.

YOU PROMISED THE BEAR, he said. YOU PROMISED ME.

You spoke with my voice, I said. You promised, and only you.

I said this, but I knew it was not true, and afterward the fingerling said nothing else, but for a time he knocked about my stomach and then the cavity of my chest and then both at once and other places besides, voice box and the clicking joint at the back of my jaw, then back down, through organs I could not feel until he hurt them, gall bladder and spleen and liver and others whose names I knew only in abstract or only when pulled from the bodies I had trapped.

The fingerling hurt me until all that remained lay prostrate on the ground, where I pleaded for him to stop, to show his father mercy, but he only twisted me worse, claimed I was no father of his—and of course if he wanted to be right, then he was right, because even if I called him my child I knew he was not, not anymore.

And in this room: The voice of the foundling as I had rarely heard it, as he talked to my wife when they were alone. A voice high and eloquent, curious and questioning, so different from the silence that blanked his wild face whenever I appeared.

And in this room: the number of times my wife hurt the foundling, even accidentally. A number so close to zero.

And in this room, the number of times the foundling touched me without fear, counted up and counted through, each enumeration instanced, made distinct: Here was the foundling wiggling his tiny fingers in his crib.

Here him clutching my then-offered finger, here him putting that finger into his mouth, biting hard.

Here the foundling crawling toward my lake-mudded boots, then his body mounted atop the mound of my foot.

Here the foundling asking me to lift him into my lap, asking me with his hands because he had not yet learned to speak.

Here the foundling pushing my hands away from his mother's, so that he might have her instead.

Here, here, here and here and here, some few others all so similar and the same, and all when the foundling was youngest and then barely ever again.

And in this room: The foundling's first step, first word, first loving profession. All the firsts I missed, away, sequestered with my own oldest son, ghost of might have been. This well-loved triptych of action, of sound, of affection—and what could our other son do in response but spit, but chew and gnaw every reach to which he found access.

And in this room: the many faces my wife had since made the foundling, shaped from the ruins of his old face, the one burned free by our final pot of stew. How she sang his flesh into new shapes, laid fresh expressions atop the face she had given him as an infant, and now he was a child remade in her own image, remade again and again until why bother with a name at all, because how would we recognize the one to whom it belonged?

In that room I said his name anyway, and even this did not go unpunished, and afterward the fingerling hissed: THE FOUNDLING, he said. THE FOUNDLING AND ONLY THAT. CALL HIM THAT, OR CALL HIM NOTHING.

AND BETTER NOTHING.

BETTER NEVER AGAIN.

And in this room: How bears will eat their young. How in the right anger or hunger, they will end what they have made, will strike it down with claw, will rend it apart with tooth. How a bear will swallow the bones that she birthed. How a bear will lick free the marrow that started within her. How a bear's fur will become matted with blood that it once shared, umbilical, placental, pumped heart to heart.

And in this room: the argument that no woman would do such a thing, nor any man.

And yet this fingerling swallowed into my stomach; and yet this punishment and parenthood spread between my bones.

—

And in this room, in this whole final series of rooms, something else, not memory but prophecy, or else memories of the future, of the people we would be when we arrived there, or as perhaps we had already arrived, in a world where so much was made to circle, to roundabout: Her, asleep in a burning bed. Her, fevered beyond recognition. Her, waiting for me to reach her chambers. Her, not caring if I ever did or else not able to care. Her, happy with her foundling and then sending the foundling away. Her, dead or dying but only if I did nothing.

So much of what I saw there was only possibility made flesh and space, made room and what goes inside a room: all this purity of potential, all this stripping down to the elements, and now the eleventh element, named long after it had become all I had, all I hoped to see.

There were twelve elements, and the eleventh was called *memory*.

Memory, as all the earth was filled with, as all our bones.

Memory, an element breaking and taking apart the others, storing them away.

Memory, so that even after the other elements were gone they were still there, so that even after they were used up they were already returning.

HOW LONG I SEARCHED FOR her, and how many more rooms I entered, and as I searched how my beard widened its dishevelment, how my fingernails grew longer and more yellowed, caked beneath with dirt, with some rare fish and fowl stolen from memory-lake, from mystery-woods. How the years passed, and how much older I was after, and how rarely hungry anymore, full anyway with the stuff of my taking, with what the bear had put inside me.

How next my muscles slipped waxy down my bones. How my hair faded, star white as my wife's eyes after they paled with her sadness, after the making of the moon and the coming of the foundling. How with no seasons there was only watch-time left to track, a circle circling circles, that mechanism passed down by my father, which had marked all the hours of his marriage until he gave it to me, at the beginning of mine.

How then my watch stopped.

How something like years passed, even with no record, and still I climbed farther downward into the deep house, into its spires plunging into the depths of the earth, until at last there were no more rooms, no more passageways, only a chamber that led to the landing at the top of a great stairs, of a series of steps spiraling into a blackness that my sight could not penetrate or pierce.

Into a *black*, the twelfth and final element, into which I would not go.

Into a black, which unlike all the other elements had no twin I then knew upon the surface, between the dirt and the sky.

The black, awful as it was, I believed then it could be found only in caves, in lakes, at the bottom of houses, and who knew what was below it, what was waiting within?

We looked out into the darkness from atop those first widened and also taller steps, perceived the enormity yawning before us: At that depth, there was again wind, blowing up from the chasm below, and also there was something like rain, water dropping from some ceiling above, some higher height far above where the fingerling and I stood, that low spot we had descended to that was still not low enough, for it did not contain what we sought. The walls ahead were so distant as to be invisible, or else the dark was so dense that they were close but not knowable, and below us that bottomless black soared, and despite my long want I trembled, and so did the fingerling.

I was already an old man, skin flapping upon the flagpole of my bones, and still I waited as if there were more time coming, as if my clock were not run out. But after I grew restless I also grew brave, or at least brave enough to crawl on my belly to the dark end of that platform, to yell my wife's name down into the void.

There was no answer to my many shouts, not even an echo, and how far did the drop have to be for there to be no echo? How far away the walls?

How far away my wife?

The fingerling claimed that even if she had descended these stairs into the black, she could not have survived the cold and darkness I felt from below, nor whatever worse world surely lay at such a bottom, and as I lay there, lacking the will to go on, my belly upon the freezing stone, I felt each tensile moment stretch, closed my eyes as if to sleep. But then I did not sleep, could not against the pain that followed, as the fingerling divided himself again and again, found unclaimed organs to inhabit, new stations from which to weave a plan, one befitting my increased cowardice, and when at last he spoke his voice was newly deeper, aged as I had aged.

He said, IF YOUR PURSUIT IS ENDED, THEN IT IS TIME FOR US TO LEAVE.

For an age I ceded some sliver of control, then more and more, so that I would not always have to think of what I'd done, what I knew he would compel me soon to do. And then to pretend that I could turn back, once I had stepped even one foot upon that path, but not to have to pay for my mistake, not quickly, and always to carry this reminder, this memory as an inversion of responsibility: To no longer want to fish for fish or trap for mammals. To no longer want to eat at all. To be so old already, and to feel my long life heavy upon me, upon the body that was not quite mine now that the fingerling had aged too, so that from the womb of my stomach he might grow into a ghost the shape and size of a man, or else many ghosts assembled in the shape of the same, and in my frustrated despair I let this ghost lead us upward, away from the great stairs, toward the trapdoor miles above, at the back of our first cellar, that threshold that I hoped might still exist. And also to know that it was not the father who was supposed to take orders from the son. To know that it was not the son who was meant to show the father how to exist in the world, how to be one with the qualities of its elements.

If only I had been stronger.

If only I had not pretended to believe his lie, that his plan would smoke her out, would again return her to the surface, where I might more easily beg of her what I wished to beg.

If only that, then not this: Together the fingerling and I left that landing, ascended until we reached the next-highest floor, the deepest of the deeper rooms, the last proper chamber before the climb down to the landing atop the great stairs.

There we moved as one, acted together in deed no matter how separate our reasons, and together we took kit and kindle from my satchel, sparked flames to light one of the last torches we had brought, and with it we set fire to one room after another, until the flames spread to all the deep house my wife had made, the house she had made for me.

THE SLATE AND STONE OF the walls refused to burn, but in between there were plenty of shapes that would, and so the deep house was emptied. Soon my fingers streaked and burned with the hot pitch of my torches, and if I had only begun to cough before, now I started again, my body often bent and stalled, jerking against the smoky walls of my wife's hallways until my lungs were cleared enough to go on. When I could walk again I continued to light my fires, and as I moved away from their consumption I climbed always upward, through the rising smoke. At last I crouched along some smallest passage, and at its end I found a ladder that led to a trapdoor, an entrance to the house not previously used. Behind me I could see the flames following, and so I did not hesitate, did not turn back to look for the entrance I had previously used: With what haste I could muster I climbed past the trapdoor's sung hinges to stand into the original cellar of our house, that cubed dirt lined with long-rotted tubers and dusty jars of what had once been fruit, and although the fire had climbed behind me it did not yet burst through. For a while I was afraid, not yet sure if it would, but like so many other elements of our world it seemed unable to cross over even the least threshold, this trapdoor's lip up from the deep house. For some time the smoke still exited that hole and also some others, and its heat persisted for many months, a danger also made some grace, for that heat warmed the house that otherwise would have been so very cold, too frozen to hope to hold our happy living.

Returned to the house I had built, I found its rooms as empty of wife and foundling as ever, and also newly damaged, shattered upon their frames: Unguarded, our house had been visited by the bear, whose footprints now circled the house, and I found the windows smashed in by her blows, the logs of our walls tortured loose from their studs. Everywhere there was loosed fur and dried snot marking the house as no territory of ours, and then I knew what I should have suspected, that she had tried to follow us down into the deep house, that if she had fit through any of the openings leading below, then surely we would have seen her there.

What foolishness it was to return, I told the fingerling. What danger you have put us both in, and still we are no closer to your mother, to the better son that clings to her side.

To prove he could, he tortured me for my words, pressed in upon all the many nerves now at his command—and so our climb was ended by this homecoming celebrated only with weeping upon my knees, with beating my fists against the cursed dirt I found waiting outside the house, with hurling my voice at the moon-bent sky, its tortured gossamer hanging lower now than ever before.

ACROSS THE TREE LINE FOR the first time in years or decades, in perhaps some other longer length unreckonable as all time then was, I arrived there unprepared for the changes visited upon the woods, how its low spaces choked with rough-edged hedges, with brambles and thickets, so that all my old passages were no more. With some effort I reached the burying ground, and found within it the last fallow patch beneath the boughs and thorns, last remnant of my small incursion upon the land of the bear, where still nothing fresh would grow.

My traps had been set according to the dictates of experience and long routine, but with this new arrangement of scrub and thorn I could not easily find where I'd placed them. Warily at first, then bolder as over some days the bear failed to appear, I began to hack through the denseness of the brush until I thought I had found each trap, including some still containing the bones or part of the bones of some animal caught long ago, in the first days after I armed the steel jaws that undid them: Here a muskrat, crumbled into tiny ribs, tiny skull, here a wolf undone the same, here a trampled otter and there some fox.

I reset my traps, and each day after I visited that dark-soiled burying ground, carrying with me some new-caught wastrel nearly bare of fur and fight, and as I interred it into the cold, hard dirt, I checked again the newer graves I had earlier dug. None had been disturbed, and still there was no bear nor even any sign of her, and as I cut new paths through the trees I found I could not even find my way back to her cave, that entrance with which I was once so familiar. For a time I began to imagine that the bear had passed away in my long absence from the dirt and the woods and the lake, but the fingerling did not believe it, did not let me believe.

Long before, I had professed a belief that what a man did for his wife was to build her a house, and so in the absence of the bear and my unwillingness to leave I made some move to rebuild what had been broken, what worn-out house remained. The smoke from below had grown less strong, and the dirt even colder, and so I wrapped myself in new furs uncured and still smelling of the woods, then crossed the tree line to knock down some fresh trees from which to cut logs for our walls. It took some manner of days to drag each across the dirt, and by the time I had some sizable number beside the crooked house I realized I no longer remembered how I'd built it, or else what I did remember did not apply to rebuilding. With nothing else to do I moved from dirt to lake to woods to house to cellar, where often when I could not sleep I sat above the trapdoor to the world below, breathing in the fading smoke-smell and expelling it back out, calling my wife's name down into the dark, a repetition of my cowardice atop the great stairs, repeated until my breath came slower and harder, until my voice was choked silent, my lungs packed with the fingerling's thick shapes, their oily jelly.

Even with the house's slivered walls punched full of holes it was still warmer inside than out, and so I lay on the floor beside our bed, that better shape broken by the bear's frustrated blows or else some collapsing portion of our house's roof, and there I made myself a nest of old furs, all stale smelling but no worse off than I had left them, with no moths or rats living upon the barrenness of the dirt to chew their hides. Through the gaping roof I watched the two moons, and the rooms of the house flickered with the weird days and the long nights and their heavy glow, their differing shafts of damp light filtered by the splinters of our struts and beams.

The sky was so close then, and without stars or clouds I could see how far it had bent, at how sharp an angle it now rested, encumbered by the extra bulk of my wife's barely aloft construction. The dirt and the house were silent, except for the wind bearing the creaking sounds of the strained curvature above, and I wondered how long we would be safe there and also if, when her moon fell, my wife and the foundling would be saved beneath the dirt, or the bear within her cave.

And then one night there came another creak.

And then on another night, another.

And then some other night when the fingerling said, IT IS TIME TO FLEE THE DIRT, TO RETURN TO WHERE YOU ONCE CAME FROM.

IT IS TIME TO TAKE ME TO THE OTHER SIDE OF THE LAKE, AND OVER THE MOUNTAINS BEYOND, WHERE YOU WILL CEASE, WHERE YOU WILL RELEASE ME, WHERE I WILL LIVE AND LIVE AND LIVE IN YOUR STEAD. AND SO AT LEAST SOME PART OF YOU WILL GO ON.

And that night I sat heavy with his words, and sometime later the buzzing sky begin to crack from its burden, forked everywhere with lightning that flashed across its surface but then did not disappear, instead remaining through the accompanying thunder and then beyond, and as I wondered at the lightning's indelible persistence the fingerling spoke again.

WIFE AND FOUNDLING AND BEAR, he said, AND YOU UNABLE TO SAVE EVEN A SINGLE ONE.

And still I held my stubborn position, as always I had meant to hold it.

THE SMOKE FROM THE DEEP house stopped, and afterward everything turned to ice, all the world except the lake, its salted surface, and how long my life might have persisted like that, with me waiting white bearded and bent of body, if not for an injury worse than any other I had suffered: Cutting my way through the new and thicker brush of the woods, I stupidly put my foot into one of my own traps, its mechanism concealed beneath the undergrowth, and then I was caught by that forgotten device, some snare that the fingerling had failed to warn me away from, as he had warned me from so many others.

The snapping clasp of the trap's mechanical jaws caught me by the ankle, breaking the skin and cutting muscle and tendon, and as the pain burned through my stuck leg I howled as so many other beasts had howled, screamed my accusations, screamed out my anger at the fingerling. At last he hoped to be proved stronger than me, and how I feared he was, all his smirking shapes together perhaps at last a better ghost than I was a man.

———

To plan the sawing of knife through bone, but again to fail to commit. To wail and drag at my broken, bloody leg, hauling the chained trap behind me in some limited circle, but to hear no response except the same silence that had already filled that frozen wood.

To despair, but to keep my feet, because to sit down upon the ice-strewn ground would be the first step toward giving up, toward accepting the death the fingerling had led me into, or else the begging for my life he hoped would win him his desires.

To sit down anyway, because eventually there was no strength left for the standing.

To feel my breathing shallow, my pulse slow. To close my eyes, and see nothing except the fingerling's clumping movements inside my head, behind my eyes, his dark sparks and darker flashes.

To hear nothing, and then after the nothing at last something new, and then the fingerling's agitated voice, saying NO, saying NO, saying NOT HIM.

To open my eyes to spy the approaching foundling, that boy who had never before been brave enough to cross the tree line, who had so rarely wandered even that far without my wife making soft tracks behind him, now trudging toward me through the bracken and the bramble, at last unafraid of the woods or else made the master of his fear.

I struggled, staggered to what remained of my feet, and then I called out to the foundling, said, We do not have much time.

I said, You should not be here, in these woods.

I said, Get out, and then I said it again and then again, and with each repetition of my warning the foundling recoiled but did not retreat, and also the fingerling raged furious, hardened his grip around my already-pressed organs, and still I tried to speak, croaking each breathless word, each syllable tasting of bile, of rotten teeth and ghosted flesh.

Help me, I said.

I said, Help me, but hurry.

The foundling I'd known was merely a child and might not have had the strength to open the jaws of the trap. This foundling was not so differently shaped, still small despite the decades passed between us, but he had little trouble yanking loose my injured leg, and if he was not careful he was at least quick, and if he hurt me worse at least I was cleared of what steel had caught me.

My ankle looked no better once freed, its bones and muscles and flesh sorely wrecked, but whatever pains the foundling caused were far less than how the fingerling would have seen me hurt, and also shamed and broken, and when the foundling stepped underneath my armpit I flinched so abruptly I nearly fell again—because what would the fingerling do now—and also how long had it been since anyone had touched me, since any other had tried to help?

With the foundling's body supporting me—he was hard and wiry then, muscled like a man despite his prepubescent shape—we stumbled slow through the brambles, then out the woods, across the tree line, toward the house. As we crossed the dirt, I saw that the foundling's once-burned face was somehow again unmarked, but also that he remained not quite well, and so he was joined to our family in this other way, how in each of us there dwelled some sickness, some scarred tissue or flustered potential, turned bone, twisted muscle: For the foundling, there was some fever found in the deepest reaches of the house, wet lands I had not seen. Or maybe it was the fire itself, caught in his flesh as it was so recently caught in the rooms of the deep house, the palace my wife had made, the ruins to which I'd had those rooms reduced.

———

Inside the house, I wrapped my already-swollen, bruised ankle in torn furs, the only bandages I could make. The inner hides filled fast with pooling blood, but I did not change them immediately, as first I thought to deal with the foundling, whose own illness seemed more pressing. There was no proper bed big enough to lay him upon, but there was my nest of blankets beside the broken one my wife and I had shared, and so I took him into the bedchamber, where I stripped off his sodden clothes, then wiped his body dry with the cleanest of our rough cloths. It took me aback to see how little he had changed against how old I had become, how heavy the decades lay upon my bones, and then I was startled again, at how passive his face remained while I toweled him, the found-ling standing dispassionate, a child waiting beside the washtub for someone else to dress him.

In the absence of clocks I did not know how long it had been since the day the foundling's mother took him away, but however many decades it had been his shape had aged only unto the cusp of adolescence: His shoulders and chest were still those of a boy, and there was no hair upon his lips or cheeks, nor under his arms or between his legs. Even the long, uncut hair upon his head was thin, thinner than I remembered, and as I stroked it off his hot face the fin-gerling made another heat inside my hands, a prickling numbness that took with it some portion of my senses there, so that I could not feel anymore the texture of the boy's skin—and yet what little I felt I clung to, and did not forget: the foundling, a boy preserved by the devices of my wife, by her voice, her voice's song.

Despite his fever, I covered the foundling in what other blankets I had, then took my bucket down to the lake, hobbling all the way,

and fetched it full of the lake's freezing water. Back in the bedroom, I found the boy asleep, his face senseless, his tossing body
turning the sheets as I tried to quiet his movements with one hand
so I could apply cool cloths with the other. Soon the room smelled
wetly of sickness and salt, and despite the deep pain in my other
joints I thanked the fingerling for my numb fingers, which could
not feel the near ice of the lake water dripping from their age-
spotted joints, and all the while that other son churned in my gut,
overflowed my stomach with his bile, flooded my intestines with
barely held diarrhea, filled my eyes with cruddy tears—and how I
ached as he pushed his shapes outward, bulged my skin to make
more room for his rage, his accusations, his righteous claims of
dominion.

How I fought him then as I had not since the burning of the
deep house.

How I fought him limb by limb, digit by digit, so that he might
not bring harm to the foundling, but to do so not yet for the foundling's sake, or not his sake alone.

Soon old hurts began to throb, and also there was my shattered
ankle, which I unwrapped and studied by the light of the moons.
I spent what water remained washing the wound somewhere out
back of the house, where thick clots and then new blood puddled
the frozen earth. What remained beneath was almost too wrecked
to call an ankle, and never again did I walk straight or stand per-
fectly upright, but when my ankle was as clean as it could be, I
wrapped it in fresh fur, making myself a boot as I had once made
an armor.

Afterward I returned to the house, to the bedroom inside the
house where the foundling slept, where he would sleep for some
long period, during which I would keep some close vigil, during

which I would leave him only twice: once to remove him something to eat from the woods, and once more to return to where the foundling had found me, so that I might drag some branches behind me, obscuring the smaller footprints he left in the blood-thawed earth nearby, so that if the bear did still live I might believe she would not so easily find his sign.

The foundling was awake again when I returned to the house the second time, sweating and shaking but able to stand and speak, his voice as high and lilting as ever. He complained of his long hunger and of the dirt's cold air, and when I pressed him to speak of his mother instead or at least first, he only repeated his complaints. In response I dressed him in my old clothes, and where those fit wrong I modified them with my knife, holding the cloth away from his body so I might slice some strips from the bottom of his shirt, from the low hem of his trousers. Afterward I sat him down at the table, and there I opened him a hairless rabbit to eat, warmed it as best I could.

While he ate I watched his face for the fear I had expected to see, but now he seemed unafraid of this room in which his features had been undone, perhaps because his face was no longer exactly that same face, not that of the son my wife had masqueraded before me, no longer a blend of my features and hers. Now I was removed altogether, by the same method by which my wife had smoothed his scars, by the way long before that she had removed the many aspects of the bear.

After he was finished, the foundling got down from his seat, came over to stand before mine, and as he placed his hand into the wiry nest of my beard, all my body quivered toward his touch. I opened my arms with more hesitance than I wished, but he did not hesitate, only climbed into my lap, curled against my chest.

He was too big to hold like this, but it was what I wanted, and anyway he was asleep before I could push him away, and as I held him, daring not to move, again and always the fingerling howled, accused, called me traitor. And did I bother to answer?

No, I did not, for what other answer was there that he would accept?

WHEN THE FOUNDLING NEXT AWOKE, I fed him the rest of his rabbit, then worked the warped iron of our stove to heat him some water, found him soap to bathe away the last of his fever smell.

I waited while he scrubbed and dried and dressed, and then I begged him to speak, to tell me of his mother, of my wife.

I said, Tell me it all, and do not stop, no matter what you see upon my face or what I do with my hands.

I said, I am not always in control of who I am, but I do not want you to be afraid of me, not anymore.

The foundling nodded, and then he said he knew, that he had long known.

He said, My mother showed me the man you used to be. She made many rooms to show me, and also to show you, so that when next we were together you would be yourself again, your right self, and we would not have to be afraid.

He said, She made a house for you, put all of herself inside it for you to recognize, but even after you saw what she wanted to say still you never came to where we were, although often we thought that you would.

He said — and here I heard his adult voice most, a deepness hidden within his child-shape — he said, Do you know how sad it made her to have you refuse her forgiveness? Do you know how sad it made me, to find you out in the woods, playing with your stupid traps?

The foundling and his mother had listened for my footsteps, and then my longer periods of stopping, resting or else slow consideration. He said that sometimes his mother said she heard me running, that I was moving faster now, that at last I was coming and that soon we would all be reunited.

Other times, he said, I would pause so long that they wept for fear of my death, for his mother said only the collapse of my bones could have stopped my advance, could have kept me away.

The foundling said he'd watched his mother waste herself to make the deep house, singing her bones inside out, making of her sweat salty rivers in which to cool my face and of her flesh banquet rooms in which to feast my hunger — but I remembered no such meals, and told the foundling so.

Certainly there were rooms of flies and rooms of maggots and rooms of garbage, I said. Certainly there were poison-rimmed goblets, plates powdered with pressed privet, tetanus-stilled beasts caught in rusty traps.

The foundling shook his too-small head, stopped the advance of his story.

Mother said you'd say that, he said.

He said, She said you were afraid of her, and also of me. That something had put a fear in you, and that now you were wary.

And still she said we should wait for you to arrive, still she said you would arrive transformed.

What if *deep house* was not all there was beneath the earth? What if there was *deep dirt*? What if there was *deep woods* and *deep lake*? What if my wife was then making some new world beneath the dirt, and only my cowardice atop the great stairs had kept me from reaching it, from taking part in its reconfigured elements?

What if I could become *deep father* and she *deep mother* and the foundling or the fingerling our *deep child*, and what if the whole world I had known — all that lake and dirt and house and woods and bear and what was not a bear, all that father and mother and child and ghost-child and moon and moons — what if all that was failed forever, doomed by our years of childlessness, our despair over those long years?

What if my wife had known how to leave it all behind? What if she had tried to tell me, and what if I had not listened?

EXHAUSTED OF HIS STORY, THE foundling slept in my lap, and as he slept I stroked his hair as I had stroked my wife's, as I had once hoped to stroke the fingerling's, when I still imagined he might be a boy.

And how the fingerling hated this substitution, the equivalency it suggested, and how he wished me to stop.

How he knew what I was doing, what I planned to do next, and as warning he filled me with his black feelings, attempted to rob me of my enjoyment, my small joy at this first night of new fatherhood, and with his movements he kept me even from sleep, from indulging in my exhaustion to take some simple slumber of father and son. I held the foundling, and the fingerling moved agitated within me, and soon I began to feel some dull pain in my shoulders, then my arms and hands.

A prickling, then a numbness, then the prickling again.

Soon my jaw ached, and I shifted the foundling so that I could free one hand to rub at its joint, then to clear the sweat from my forehead.

I had barely eaten since the arrival of the foundling, but now I felt like I had eaten too much, and if I could not still my stomach then I thought I would have to wake the foundling, send him to sleep somewhere else.

Last I felt the squeezing in my chest, like a fist wrapped around my heart, its grip bearing down, then letting up, then bearing down, a kind of contraction I had never before known, and at this touch I knew the fingerling's intent, recognized his goal even if he kept silent as he worked. In the years of our long cohabitation he had found his way into every part of my shape except my head and my heart, but now he moved to enter fully my centermost chamber, and I felt him move to block that pulsing organ, shaping his many bodies into some plug or plugs with which to stop me where I sat, and when his work was complete I seized in my chair, the jerking of my body so violent it bucked the foundling from my embrace.

I grappled dumbly at my chest, pounded the skin and sternum that separated my hands from my heart, and as I floundered the awakened foundling dragged me gasping from my seat and onto the rough-boarded floor of our house. I spasmed upon the boards, and soon I could not feel my pulse or my breathing, but still I sensed the fingerling everywhere now, every part of him on the move, and against him I sensed the foundling working from without, setting his hands upon my chest, his lips on my lips. And when that failed he began to speak, and then his speech turned to song, made a new music that even in my dying I knew I had never heard before.

The song the foundling sang was not just sound but also smell and sight, also touch and taste, and also light, also *not-black* – and with it the foundling drove his brother out of my center, back to my stomach, to my thigh, those first hiding places now again made far from what remained of me — and when the fingerling was secured, my body jerked upon the floor, all of me weakened and sweat soaked and in terrible pain.

But even in my pain I found a reveling, this returned life worth celebrating: For a moment all I felt was the glorious pounding of my heart, the busy way my lungs bellowed, that first breath so filling my chest with air that I thought I might never have to breathe again.

FROM UNDER THE WOODS THE bear had brought back all I had killed and buried, roaring them from the burying ground into new and uncut threads, perhaps diminished shades of their former shapes but at least not dead. That too was how I returned, lessened of some portion of my manhood, of what awful man I had been, but also of what protections the bear had given me: Soon my adrenaline faded, and then I began to wheeze, and then also to hack, until I expelled some number of dark clots onto the floor. Afterward the foundling helped me back into my chair, then sat down, crossed his legs before me. Even that short climb winded me, and in my chair I gasped for air, clutched at my chest. The pain radiated everywhere except the places the fingerling had been driven, and in those holdings numbness prevailed.

Despite some lingering nausea, I felt the fullness of my appetite return, a ravening long ago put aside, now returned to announce my restored need, and then suddenly I realized the foundling was speaking and that I had not been listening. I pulled myself straighter, then slumped again, placed my elbows unsteady upon my knees, let my head tilt to one side or the other. From that stance I could not see the foundling's face well, and as he talked I struggled to understand the words he made, his stuttered syllables high pitched and softly spoken. I asked him to start again, to speak slowly until this story was told, the only story that had ever happened to him alone: not the story of his time with my wife in the deep and deepest houses, but of his journey away from her side.

As we had burned the deep house empty so the foundling had watched his mother catch a fever she could not cool, and as she burned she diminished: her breasts flattened, her skin loosened, until she was all bones and jaundice. But still the foundling stayed at her side, and still he sometimes drank from her, for eventually there was no other food, and after what little milk my wife had left soured soon he too was sick, the fever that filled her filling him. And with each meal he took from her he had to know his mother was dying.

The hot house above burned, and as it did her skin reddened, then blistered and flaked off, and the foundling had the scars to prove it, bands of once-blistered flesh on his hands and wrists, earned smoothing back the smoking snakes of his mother's hair. When his mother could not lift her head to cry or her hands to feel, the foundling had crawled into their bed for the last time, curved his stalled bones inside the skinny ess of her own.

Cradled in that last cradle, the foundling wept, and as she burned away his tears his mother spoke.

I know your face, she said, but you are not the only one. Still there is a memory of your father, the first time I met him, which always I have held back, and if I remember nothing else I remember that.

A sweating silence followed, and some new hours of forgetting, and then she said, And I remember a bear, and also a cub crying for its mother.

I took that cub, she said, and as I carried it from a cave I used my mouth to peel off its softest fur, clump by clump.

What the foundling told me last: That when he left, my wife still remembered my name.

That she remembered at least that, if she remembered nothing else.

That she said my true name to the foundling. That she whispered its two syllables into his ear against the curve of his collarbone. That she breathed me onto his skin, gave him all the sympathetic memories she had left, so he would not be afraid as he had been, as I had made him to be.

With a final kiss, she said, I wish I would remember you after you are gone, and then she sent him away, sent him as an orphan into the world she had made—as the orphan he would become, if I would not take him in, or if I was no longer alive—and then for a while he was alone in the world, a best-loved son unremembered, climbing upward through those many miles of smoldered spires, their crumbling structures sloping in. And as he'd climbed he took into himself the miles of scorched stairs and hollowed halls, that mimicry of his mother's own interior landscape, that palace of her I had wrecked and ruined, and now with this telling he meant to give me what he had carried, so that I might be forced to carry it too.

FROM THE PILE OF CAST-OFF furs beside the house, I chose the cleanest strips to replace the dirty dressing around my ruined ankle, my trap-clubbed foot, and then I washed my face in a bucket of salt water, my hair in the same. As I moved around the outside of the house I kept my eyes on the tree line, nervous that the bear might appear there. I had not seen her since the day we fought in the woods, that same day she gave me the fur her son had once been buried inside, kept still in the satchel slung often around my body, which contained also the near-identical fur I had taken from the deep house, the only object pulled from my fire. Now I again removed the two furs from that satchel, tried to remember which was real and which only sung, and when I could not I told myself that it could not matter, this slim difference between the memory and the thing remembered.

At the most crimson hour of the dusk, I led the foundling down to the cold shores of the lake, where I put him into the rowboat and then rowed us out upon the water. As I fished for our dinner I wondered aloud if the foundling had the same strength of voice his mother had, if he could tear down the last stars, invisible behind the light of his mother's moon—or else could he buoy that red shape back up into the sagging sky, almost broken then? Since the foundling's return more cracks had appeared across the bowl of the sky, and now all the visible sky was fractured, streaked with more stuck lightning, those sights emitting their accompanying hummings and buzzings and long low thunders, and I asked him if he knew what would happen next, if his mother had told him what we should do.

But no matter what I said, the foundling said nothing in return, only sometimes shook his head or shrugged, stared off across the water. Now it seemed impossible to recall the face he had worn before, when last he was meant to be my son: Whatever song his mother had used to take him from cub to boy had perhaps blocked his progress from boy to adult, and I wondered if this could be set right, if there was some other song his mother could sing that would unbind him.

When next he lifted his eyes to mine, I pointed to the sky, and I said, Do you know what the red moon means? Or what happens next?

I said, Are you scared?

I said, In the morning we will go back. We will find your mother, and if we can help her, then we will.

The foundling still did not speak, only stared at me with his changeless face, the constellation of his eyes only two points, a single line, and yet what story I saw there, answering even without his speech to guide me: That he missed her. That if we could not find her again it might be a kindness, as he would be able to hope forever that she was not dead.

And then again I was jealous of what he had that I did not, and because I could not stop myself, I said, Everything you will lose when she dies, I have already lost.

It was the fingerling who broke the silence that followed, speaking for the first time since the night of his last attack, saying NO, saying NO again, saying THE BEAR IS COMING, THE BEAR IS COME, THE BEAR HAS COME AND SHE WAITS FOR YOU ON THE DIRT AND SHE WAITS FOR YOU IN THE HOUSE AND SHE WILL TAKE WHAT YOU HAVE KEPT FROM HER, AND THIS TIME I WILL NOT LET YOU DEFEAT HER, and what I heard also was not DEFEAT but DECEIVE, a choice perhaps, spoken in two voices.

I stopped my rowing, pulled the paddles up from the water, let the surface still around us. The air filled with our gray breath, and the shimmer of my wife's moon seemed to waver from above, and though I could not see her I heard the bear roar from the dirt, and with that roar I saw more lightning crack across the sky, and also that the lightning already frozen there had begun to move, first slowly and then quickening, sparking red and green and blue-white across the inner sphere. The bear barked, then roared again—and in that roar I heard a new sound, a naming, and where had the bear learned such a thing—and then as the bear called the red moon's name that moon began its fall, and as it burst the last skin of the sky it fractured, bursting into some innumerable flock of missiles, and each irregular shape ignited as it dropped through the atmosphere, and this time there was no wife-song, no other power waiting to save us.

THE FRACTURING MOON FELL THROUGH a cloud of sound, the racket of the sky's awful cracking, and every part of the moon's broken body arrived aflame, the first rough clumps to impact jolting the dirt into the air, and then the next wave concussed the already-broken ground, sending shock waves across the lake and also debris back toward the sky, great eruptions digging deeper craters. Above us the other moon snapped back upon the dazed ellipse of its orbit, suddenly brighter without competition, and as I watched it dance back into place I also saw how the sundered sky refused the dirt's offering, so that soon gravity returned earth to earth, ten thousand handfuls of rock and sod falling upon the dirt and the lake, and for some time both the foundling and I had to crouch and cover our heads, to protect ourselves from the last moon rocks piling up in the bottom of the boat or else splashing loudly into the water around us.

When at last it was safe I stood and found my balance and looked toward the shore, through the swirling debris and dirt clouds, and there I was sure I spied some portion of the house still standing, set upon a promontory shoved up through the cracking of the earth. Behind it I saw the woods aflame, and from those woods came again the bear, her brutish shape emerging grotesque from the fire. I could not possibly have heard her above the loud discord of the dirt's destruction, but when I saw her bared teeth and angry stance upon the shore I imagined her hoarsened sound calling across the lake, and then I lost sight of her in the confusion. A moment later I again thought I saw her fur-bare armor silhouetted against the fire, imagined the sizzle of exposed bone, that terrible pain issuing from her lungs. I watched for her where I could, but more than I wanted to know where she was, I wanted only for her to be gone, and then I saw her leaving, a blank shadow turning slowly in a sea of red flames, returning the way she had come, back into the blazing trees.

Lightning cracked above, true lightning not stuck but fresh and flashing, and the rain turned to downpour turned to storm, and upon the lake the salt water chopped, the surface rough where it had been the stillest. The foundling and I were tossed in our rowboat as I put the oars to the waves, pulled hard for shore, but we were too far out, and the water was too churned, and any begging for help I directed at the fingerling fell unanswered on his dumb lumps. Soon our route went wide of the right line to shore, and then I pounded my fists against my choked thighs, pleaded with that one son to help me save the other, regardless of their bad blood, the no blood between them, and then I roared too, until my tears and my noise frightened the foundling, frightened him as bad as the falling sky, the dark clots of flung-up dirt still crashing into the water all around, the shore collapsing into the lake even as we tried to reach it. The foundling screamed for me to stop as I screamed at the fingerling to do the same, until our voices were interrupted by the next disruption of the dirt, the second such shaking, and then some angry waves shook out across the surface of the lake, raising the rowboat high upon their crests, then dropping it down into unsteady furrows, where from its flat bottom we watched the water climb in high battlements above us, and when those battlements collapsed their cold contents filled the trough between with more water, caved wet walls crashing in.

THE EDGE OF THE OVERTURNING rowboat struck the foundling first and then me, knocking me somewhere in the back of the head or between the head and the neck, in some awkward place where I could not reach the injury, not while I kicked for the surface, and not afterward, while I struggled against the waves and searched the surface for the foundling. At last I saw him already heading toward the burning dirt, the house or house-hole remaining, and while I wanted to hurry after him I was not sure I could make it to the shore. I treaded water as best I could, but I tired fast with the drag of my new wound, and so I struggled only until his stroking form was small in the distance, close enough to shore that I could imagine his safe arrival, and then I did not try to follow.

Instead I made myself believe it was not just *whale* that inhabited our lake but another as well, the two connected by *ghost*, and for once the fingerling did not fight me but instead encouraged the story I was telling. At his suggestion I sank like a stone, like the stone of my heart, like the stone knife of the fingerling scraping at the walls of my heart, slashing toward escape, and in that passage into darkness something else shifted, for as I swam and sank and broke my chest to breathe I did not die, and around me the water seemed to be salt water no longer, not exactly, but instead both salt and water, and as I fell also again something thicker, more slippery, blacker even than the dark water, a sea of ink where once there was a lake of salt.

I threw myself ever lower, tunneled into the water at the fingerling's command, this swimming motion almost all he knew from his short life, his too-quick float in his mother's belly. All of me ached now, and still there was farther to go. I begged off, begged to rest, to quit, but then the fingerling spoke again, his heavy words dragging me down, forcing me under.

He said, IN THE WOMB, IF YOU STOPPED SWIMMING, THEN YOU DIED.

He said, ONCE, I THOUGHT THE WOMB WAS THE WORLD, AND THEN WHEN THAT WORLD REJECTED ME WHAT OTHER CHOICE EXISTED EXCEPT DROWNING, EXCEPT HOLDING MY BREATH UNTIL I BURST?

NOW DIVE, he said, and so I dove, swimming until I reached the bottom of the lake, but not the bottom of its center I had expected, only its center's edge, its near shelf, the drop-off where the safe part of the water ended, the coolness below the burning surface above, where that band of cool fell down into colder darkness. On that shelf I leveraged myself lower, and also I felt the first floating strands of gunked eggs, unfertilized and untended and half gnawed, a thousand wasted babies, food for the silver faces of the lake's fish, those blank expressions surrounding our dive, our pursuit into the thick black of the cloud below. I kicked deeper, drove our bodies down with the movement of my good leg and then my bad leg and then my good leg again, but despite my effort I did not make it to the center of the lake alone or even alone with the fingerling.

I could not have, not even before my crushed ankle or my other newest injury.

Now I knew that what still lived in the lake had many names and shapes but was then best titled *squid,* and although the bear thought it dead it was not exactly, and after its long-lashing reach hooked my skin I thought I would drown, but no, I did not die, not then.

HE COMES, said the fingerling, HE COMES AND HE IS YOU AND YOU ARE HIM AND NOW AT LAST YOU ARE BOTH HERE TOGETHER, and the fingerling's voice was a hissing threat but also quieter than any other time of late, a hush that made me more afraid, and I felt him withdraw into his stomach-pit, and then the lake's giant squid struck, reached out from the black beneath the lake to wrap me in its rough-puckered tentacles, to slash my skin with their barbed hooks.

I exhaled a scream of bubbled air, struggled to free myself even as the squid bid me to be still, fixing me with one huge eye and then the other. After some time the squid began to speak as the bear spoke, in an old language translated by the fingerling, its tentacle-shrouded beak snapping close to my face, saying that there was more to the making of a child—of a family—than just two bodies, than two bodies and an empty set of rooms.

It said, I AM LIKE YOU, BUT I AM NOT YOU, and when its voice thrashed against the sides of my skull I knew it was no real squid, only a ghost in the shape of a squid, and in my drowning I believed I smiled, and even in my stomach the fingerling laughed, as if ghosts were no danger, as if ghosts and their memories had not been the whole of our undoing.

The squid-ghost circled me in the floating blackness, and as it circled it spoke, and with words barely words, it said, YOU SEEK TO MAKE ONLY A CHILD, ONLY A HANDFUL OF CHILDREN, BUT I WANT MORE.

It said, YOU HAVE SEEN THE EGGS I KEEP, THE EGGS I TOOK FROM MY WIFE WHEN LAST SHE SWAM IN HER FIRST SHAPE.

It said, THEY ARE LESS NOW, BUT THEY ARE STILL MINE, AND STILL THEY ARE IN NEED OF A GOOD FATHER, and then it sprayed wide clouds of useless ghost semen and blackest ink, twin excretions fogging the deep lake.

It said, WHAT YOUR WIFE CANNOT MAKE, MINE ONCE REFUSED ME.

It said, AFTERWARD, I TRIED TO KILL MY WIFE AS YOU TRIED TO KILL YOURS, BUT I COULD NOT SUCCEED AS YOU HAVE, and as it said this I shook, because despite the fall of her moon I did not believe my wife was dead. And then the squid spoke again, said, KILL HER FOR ME, its tentacles drawing me close, the hard shell of its body long against me, and against its grip I shook my head, struggled again to escape.

KILL THE BEAR, the squid said. MAKE FRESH THIS WORLD ONCE AGAIN.

After I refused its offer, the squid opened my skin with its hooks and slammed its snapping beak into my chest, and even though the squid was a ghost, still it was powerful there in the lake-black: With sharp movements, it set to folding back the sheets of my skin, splitting some numbers of ribs and also the tissues between. It pushed forward, and my body bulged to accommodate its entrance, its puke-yellow eyes leading the strange wedge of its alien face, and then I was speared upon its sharp ridges, and then the fingerling was pushing back from all his holdings, and between them or upon them I was caught fast and screaming, thrashing against the squid's attack, its refusal to accept my declining of its barely bartered truce, and for a while we spiraled deeper into the depths of the lake, a black made of the squid's ink and also something else, where there was no sound and sight, where even our battle was subsumed into the silence, and where I burst against the cold and the dark until I was reduced to a held breath, a bit of bodily heat, a movement slowed and almost stopped. Still the squid-ghost swam on, not farther down but farther in, into me, trying to squirm its ghost into the spaces I contained, that space that in me was already filled with my own fractured haunts, my cancer-son, and would admit no other.

The squid's shape was so heavy, so thick with ropes of ink now pushing into me too, and as I dropped through that black I dreamed a squid's dream: I had not one child but thousands, all same faced as me, all hatching out of the lake at once, from both the egg clutch along the shelf ridge and also somehow from out of my arms, out of my legs, from out of my mouth and ears and nose, all little stars bright with tentacles and sharp black mouths, all floating upward toward the light.

The weight of the squid weighed upon me, and as I watched my dream-children swim off I sank deeper into their making, and in this dream I saw my life did not end with my death but rather went on, spread wide across the face of the world, my children a country of men and squid, so that everywhere there was lake we were there, and everywhere there was dirt there was a man sent to build his house upon it.

Throughout our fall the fingerling fought the squid from every inner space, pushed back with his many tumors, and soon the squid balked, struggled to withdraw, wriggling its barbs backward. Outside my body again, the squid swam long curves around my sinking weight, its angry shape first invisible in the black, its voice now lower than words, untranslatable even by the fingerling, and then again it was upon us, slashing with beak and claw, and as we fell, the depth's pressure squeezed my lungs until they broke further, filled with ink, burst again.

How tired I was of almost dying, of suffering the sequenced steps without release: Here was the cold, the dark, the black, all around me and inside, and here was my crooked foot and my dented head or neck and all the rest of my hook-scraped and beak-burst body, and still I did not give in, still some part of me scratched forward, succored for life, for even what sorry life I had waiting. I reached into my boot for my blade, my knife dulled with decades of skinning and scaling, and as I drowned deeper I fought back, put the single sharp edge of my blade against the squid's soft shell, and together we sank through another fathom of struggle before it tried again to whip me toward the crook of its stained beak, before I raked my knife across one tentacle and then the other, before I plunged it toward the squid's eye — that eyeball alone the size of my head — and in the dark I moved the knife into the black at the center of its glimmering iris, into and then through that ring of light, pushing the knife so deep my wrist disappeared into the shell behind, and somewhere within the knife finally caught, then wrenched from my grip in a wet squelch of ichor — and still I knew I had not ended the squid, what ghost remained of this once-father.

Not to have killed it but to have at least made half of it dark.

To have at least made that half *black*, blacker, and then to have that part and others broken, made a scrim swimming all around me, a body floating like a shroud.

MEMORY AGAIN AS TRANSFORMATION, AS transfiguration: to swim or else float or fall inside the tearing-apart, to be joined with this squid-thing, this whale-thing, this desperation that could be either a squid or a whale, that in one of its shapes the bear had ended. And still it went on, and amid my dispersal swam the squid's anger, its own remainder, fury at how it could not enter my cavity, and if it could not claim the inner chambers of my body, at least it could reshape the shell.

The fingerling was already familiar with this squid's motion, swimming and tentacled and inky black, and I was made that swimmer's shape too, and soon my breathing stopped being one kind and became another, and by that change I finally came to believe what I had been told: that despite our too-many numbers there were always only two, and that those two begat no true offspring, because it was always the same two that appeared, in this and in every age, and yet everywhere on this dirt there were too many.

FTERWARD, WHAT OTHER POWER LED me up through the shallower lake, what glowing guide except the light of the moon? Not my wife's moon, shattered and fallen, but that other again made lonely above the earth, its long light cutting even the ink-water of the new lake, making floating ribbons shimmering around this new body, shorn and reshaped, this face different now beneath the water than it had been above.

As I ascended, the fingerling taught me the motions this shape necessitated, the jetting this way and that, choosing a path zigzagged upward through the layers of coldest and then colder and then just cold. For a long time, he urged me to stay away from the surface, but I did not understand his hesitance until after I burst the plane between salted ink and rain-soaked air: Beneath the water I would always be squid, would take on the role hollowed out for me by the long-ago aggression of the bear, but above I would for some time longer be only myself, only failed husband, broken father.

At first I waited there, tried to be both, to have both, but the fingerling denied me, pushed me to pick. NO, he said. YOU CANNOT ALWAYS WANT TO HAVE EVERYTHING.

Diving back through the lake, I snatched at schools of fish and passing eels, feastings for me and my son, and as my new shape swelled, the fingerling swam within me; his shapes changed too, constrained by my shifting, and for some time we moved together, and after our hungers were satisfied I began our gradual shearing of the surface, and when we broke again the plane of the lake's surface it was to find the rain softened, the wind reduced, the waves manageable even in the dark, the first true dark in many years. From the surface I searched the shoreline with my human eyes, then as the squid I dove below to swim in toward the shallows, on the way checking the shelf and what lay between the shelf and the shore for any sign of the foundling, finding none except some scent of his blood, some taste of his vomit, and also of salt and fish and bile reduced, traces I imagined discernible only to my new and watery senses.

And then for a moment not to care so much about the foundling, at least not the foundling as a boy, which was not the shape of son my new shape craved.

And then to want to swim back into the depths, the deep and deeper lakes where my body would stay as perfect as any other swimming creature's, at last ideal for what activities I would put it to, evolved right.

All I had to do was choose the lake over the land forever, and then I could be a new thing, a squid first and a whale after, and for a moment I knew how the one who came before me had arrived at his station, and also what he had traded to claim it.

And how sorely I was tempted, ready then to return to whatever waters, to linger in the naked dark with the black and inky salt around my ruined ankles, as I did after I first stood into the cold air, watching the squidness slip free of my body—but it was only by choosing the land that I could choose my wife, and so what other choice could I make, what else but to once more become a man.

T**HOSE DAMNED AND CLOCKLESS HOURS.** Those unrecordable days, their tricky times, unable to be measured or even to have their passing discerned, and still some events did happen, still some progressions ran onward, unchecked and uncontrolled: Now the dirt crawled with flames, hot tongues licking that old star-glass, melting some into a form again slippery, still malleable and undetermined as I walked ashore, carrying the shape of a squid inside me, and also the many bodies of the fingerling, who I knew had neither forgiven me nor given up his vengeance. The rain continued to fall upon us as it had before, but no longer was there as much lightning and thunder in the air, and I wondered, How long had I been beneath the water, if that storm had passed, and how would I ever know?

In the distance—up the path from the lake, up the opened hill— there I saw the ruins of our house, barely rooms, barely chimney. The moonfall had cracked its foundations and cratered the rest, and I had to step lightly across our now-treacherous yard and our rubbled sitting room to find a sure path to traverse, some way to reach the center of the house, where our rooms now fell away into the earth. I crawled out toward the edge on my hands and knees, then looked downward from that precipice into the dirt, into the rooms and hallways exposed below. That first level was damaged too, its chambers cluttered with the house's fallen furnishings, those dishes and furs and furniture, but from my vantage that sung floor still seemed more whole than the house I had built, and perhaps safe enough to enter, as I still planned.

From there I walked out of the house and then searched all around the cracked crater where the largest portions of the moon had fallen, but along its circumference I saw no good signs: On the lake side of the crater there was ink staining the soil and the water, and opposite that there was only the burned earth and ash-trees where the woods had farthest reached, and none of its animals were left where I could see them, if left at all. Occasionally I found the melted steel of some trap, and between its snapped jaws nothing remained, the fire having immolated what could not run, and no matter how many laps I made there was still no sign of the foundling, whom I had last sensed in the water, and there only faintly. Of all the elements of our world, it was mostly the woods that resisted the cooling of the falling rain, and there the clouds of ash and smoke and falling branches still thickened, so that all I could hear was the crackle of flames, the dropping of deadening limbs. Among the trees the sensed world shrunk, became some few feet of touch and taste, all dark, all ash, reddish-brown and brownish-red. There I called the foundling's name, and then that confused air entered my lungs, made me hack and cough, put bright flecks across my vision, and still I tried to hold right the path toward my memory of the cave, a path straightened by fire and missing trees, by the removal of all the brush and thorny bramble that had thwarted my last attempt to find its entrance.

And still I was lost, still I could not find what I was looking for, until again the fingerling pointed the way, turned my steps toward what he must have somehow known we would find: the entrance to the cave, and then the foundling found again, just inside that smoke-filled hole; found trying to reach one mother or another by a path less-often taken, as if all caves led to the same chambers; found by stumbling over his stilled form, my feet tangling across his empty shape to send me sprawling.

Memory as discovery of this almost son of mine, of the body: To scramble back to standing, and then to return to my knees to dig the foundling's shape from the cave floor, from what ash had already blanketed his form.

To uncover with my fingers the absence of breath, of speech or movement, and to put my hands to his chest, to push and pump and pry but to be able to add no breath or heartbeat, as he had so recently added mine to me.

To wipe away the silt and wonder again how long I had been gone, and where else the foundling had wandered before reaching the cave.

To taste what came out of his mouth and to find not life but ash and more silt, the gray stuff of his suffocation.

To cradle his body against mine and then to stand with his limp heaviness hung upon my frame.

To have forgotten the weight of a child and to regret the forgetting — but then to never forget what happened next, how it felt when my fingers discovered the wounds upon his back, the teeth marks splitting the skull, and to understand it was not the thicker air that killed the foundling but his mother the bear.

THE FIRE WAS MOSTLY EXTINGUISHED by the time we emerged from the cave, although its effect remained in its additions of ash and char, and also its reductions, its destructions of leaf and needle, of fowl and flora. When I reached the tree line I saw the dirt was no less changed, the air warmer than before, and as I watched, a soft rain continued to fall in some places, although not in all. The weather—which had for so long been only one state—was not yet righted, and various kinds of precipitation fell upon me as I carried the foundling toward the crater's edge, toward the cracked and broken house that hung above.

Between my steps aftershocks shook the ground, nearly rocked me from my feet, belied any delusions of safety I might have harbored now that the fire was gone, now that the sky's ashy gradient moved quickly toward a more recognizable hue of gray. I advanced upon the ruins of the house, which despite its rearrangement remained mostly where I had built it: All my past steps were easily remembered, and those were the paths that led me home that day, with the foundling in my arms, the fingerling mad with happiness at his false brother's new lack of everything, his body empty of all that life the fingerling had once begrudged.

All that remained was the shape my wife had given him, the body of a boy, the face that was my wife's face, if she had been a boy herself, and how it wrenched me to look upon those features. My wife had sent the foundling into my care, and I had failed her, and for that I was sorry, and for that I would descend again the deep house so that I might reach the great stairs at its bottom, that deeper house that spiraled and soared below, and I tried to convince myself that this time I would walk those steps down into the black, through that last element and then beyond, into whatever deepest house was built there, the chamber in which my wife or else the body of my wife had so long been waiting.

THE WALLS ANGLED INWARD UPON their foundations, with only the brought brick of the chimney still mostly upright, and the rest of the house swayed, its creaking caught in the inconsistent gales that blew across the dirt. From there the path into the house was not the path I had previously taken but some other raised walkway left solid or nearly solid as the ground around it had crumbled, exposing the first levels of the deep house even as their rubble filled the empty rooms within, burying some number of the scorched stone floors. I did not look down more than I had to, and in any case the carried foundling made it hard to see where I placed my feet, and with each step the fingerling continued to cry, WHY BOTHER, WHY BOTHER, WHY BOTHER. Where before he'd had to swim from muscle to muscle, from gland to organ and back again, now his presence was persistent, his movements known everywhere always, as soft lumps between the thin bones of my hand, as more-fibered protuberances upon my femur and my clavicle. My stomach, his first home, swelled with him, so that when I pissed and shat his sign was there too, in thick dark blood, in veiny clods that dislodged only when I pushed and pushed. One of my eyes now failed intermittently, alternated cloudy and dark and starry and clear, and in this too I sensed his doing, just as I did in the ringing tinnitus of my ears and the crackle of my arthritis. Always now the fingerling made himself known, as perhaps I made myself known inside him, long ago, when I had inserted a fragment of myself into the egg, the vessel of his first long float, and if half the fingerling was made of some half of me, so now half of me was made of the same proportion of him, a weight balanced inside a weight.

Or else it was only old age that I felt. And here was the proof I would not live forever, as always I'd imagined I would.

The wall near our front door held mostly solid, but others were punched through by the bear, her blows driven by that powerful hump upon her shoulders, or else ripped off their studs by moon rock and quake debris, and also singed by fire, by unstuck lightning. Even the parts of the house that had suffered no direct damage were wind worn, weather sick, and I stepped carefully across the floors as I carried the foundling's wet and filthy body into the house, lifting him through the wreckage of tables and chairs, of pots scattered and utensils flung against and sometimes through walls.

Around us the house sighed and swayed, wood groaning against grain, and above us the sky continued its sucking sound, slower now but still wheezing against the tear the moonfall had made. I carried the foundling across the wrong-angled floors and into our bedroom, where upon the bed were still the sheets where my wife and I had once lain in the hopes of making our own children, and now those lengths and widths of fabric became instead a shroud: I wrapped the foundling in that once-white cloth, given to us on the day of our wedding, and as I locked the fabric with careful folds

I remembered all of those wedding guests—my parents, the parents of my wife, our uncles and aunts and cousins and brothers and sisters, our friends when we still had friends—and for the first time I thought how they were surely mostly dead, passed away without our notice, lost twice to us because we were too far away to see or hear enough to grieve, too isolated to have any community to share with us its news. We had come to a place where all we could see was ourselves and also each other, and I had almost forgotten that there were ever others, others besides my wife and me, our fingerling and our foundling, the bear and the squid and the smaller lives over which they ruled.

I had seen in the deep house my wife's memories of her parents—of what one parent had done to the other—but also of what good people they had seemed before. I had no best memories of my own family, had always stood separate from those who were meant to stay close to me, whom I was meant to stay close to, and now maybe they were all dust, and only I was still alive. Everywhere I went I *remained*, and going with me was only the fingerling nested within, and also the dead foundling, this son to carry downward, inside, and through some fire-wrecked memory, that lost reminder of our lives as they were at the last moment of our shared past.

Only when the foundling was right-shrouded did I leave his side, and then merely to seek some pair of breeches, an old shirt my wife had sewn, plus my spare pair of boots, one-half of which I had to cut to fit my mangled foot. I gathered supplies for making light and fire, then an older knife, not my skinning blade lost in the lake but one meant for cooking, last used for the removal of fish tumors, and I packed my satchel with the two furs, the foundling's first skin and the twitching memory of it, and also my watch, that gift which I had not worn since it stopped working long before, during my previous descent. These were all the possessions I thought I needed, all I still cared to have with me, and if other objects in that house had once held meaning then they no longer did, not for me.

The house I had built was at first small, just a few rooms, a small number of windows, a single hallway and a very finite and planned-for number of doors, and all of that was still there, if also dashed apart. After I finished my preparations I walked that first house once more, examined again its remains, peered through its broken walls and windows at the dirt beyond, and everywhere I looked I saw only some element I had been cured of wanting, and as I examined the future of this world I found I no longer craved its ownership. Now I would leave it behind to again journey beneath the earth, to again search out my wife—and whether I found her or not I thought perhaps I would never return to this dirt where we had lived, nor any of the lands beyond it.

Below the limits of the house, I knew my wife's nested structure was far greater, extending even past what I had seen on my last descent. Surely the bear already roamed somewhere among those rooms, waiting between the surface and the great stairs, mad with what she had done, what I was sure she would claim I'd made her do. Soon I would be on my way to meet her, and when I did it would be with the shrouded death of her cub in my arms, with the skins of his first-meant childhood strapped to my back, and I did not yet know what I would say when next we met.

And how I would have to be ready.

And how when I lifted the foundling into my arms, the finger-ling objected, saying, OR JUST THROW IT IN THE LAKE.

And how I never would be ready.

ABANDON IT IN THE WOODS OR IN THE GARDEN OR IN THE ROOMS OF THE HOUSE.

And how I had never known what right thing to say or do, to her or to anyone else.

I DO NOT CARE WHERE YOU LEAVE IT, he said. BUT DO ANYTHING BUT BRING IT ALONG.

And how when that meeting came I would speak and act anyway, as always I had done before.

EVERYWHERE THERE WAS THE CHAR and charcoal of our ruined wedding presents, of the memory of them, and also pools of rainwater and clods of sod and fallen walls and piled rubble. I picked through those first unceilinged rooms, then the darker halls below, curious for what remained, but so little held any useful shape or other dimension that soon we moved on, downward and farther in, through room after room, and though I did not forget their contents I also did not linger long between their walls.

And in this room, a silence that had once been a song.

And in this room, a light that had once been lightning.

And in this room, a heat that had once been a fire.

And in this room, a lump of silver that had once been a ring, two rings.

And in this room, the taste of burned hair. And in this room, its smell.

—~—

And in this room, the carapaces of bees, long ago emptied.

And in this room, a wine bottle, full of the leavings of maggots but not maggots.

And in this room, a broken bowl of mirrors, reflecting nothing.

And in this room, a filthy red ribbon, for putting up a woman's hair, for tying it back.

And in this room, unwashed seeds split by fire, revealing the expectant sprouts inside, now doomed and dried.

And in this room, a sensation like the slight give of a bruised thigh, when pushed in upon by a thumb.

And in this room, a sound that might have been my wife's voice, just too far off to hear.

And in this room, a chunk of moon rock, still hot, and above it a shaft of light lifting five stories to a jagged hole in the surface, to the other moon's light pouring down.

And in this room, the spokes of a bassinet, a blanket buried beneath a caved-in ceiling.

And in this room, a trowel stained dark, used once for digging twice.

—~—

And in this room, a rag, brown with blood, with layers of old blood.

And in this room, the sound of a star hitting the earth.

And in this room, the louder sound of a moon, of part of a moon.

And in this room, a staleness of spilt milk.

And in this room, the slime and the scales of rotted fish.

And in this room, the broken body of a deer, twisted upon itself, legs over head and around antlers, and some of the rest wrenched free for feed.

And in this room, a heavy line arced in the ash, acrid urine, another marker that the bear had raced ahead, and in the next room a runny shit, fresh from her body, and how I shivered to see it, to smell it stinking still.

And in this room, somehow a baby rabbit, alive, shaking in its fur. It had perhaps come into the deep house during the firestorm above, and now it was near death, with no mother to care for it and no food to find. I was hungry too, and just as lonely, and as I picked up the trembling bunny, I wondered if I had it in me to end early one of this world's last things, so that I might go on a little longer.

I wondered, and as I wondered I stroked away the rabbit's shivers, and then I wondered no more.

And in the next deepest room, only ash.

And in the room after that, only more of the same.

And then ash in the next room and in the next room and in the next, all rooms filled with ash and smoke-marred stones still radiating heat or else steaming with water falling through cracked ceilings, through ruptured floors, and throughout that descent the fingerling kept silent his counsel, spent his energies tormenting my body instead of my mind, seizing new stations as I slept in slanted doorways and damp hallways. Then visions of battle all night. Then one morning waking to find my right leg paralyzed straight, the muscles needed to flex it away from its numb position unresponsive even as I felt some ineffective ghost kicking, some shade of the right movement. As I kneaded the muscles and cursed my stubborn son, I felt the silent smirk of his faceless form move, and I stopped my massaging to punch his shapes, not caring that I would only bruise the surface of my stomach and thighs, never harming his holdings beneath.

Let my leg go or do not, I said. I will go on no matter what you do, no matter how it might hurt.

The fingerling did not respond, only let me struggle, believing he could convince me to abandon my last charge, the foundling's body. But I would not and said as much: If I could not have carried the foundling, then I would have dragged him in his sheets, would have crawled the burned wreckage to search out enough wood to make a sledge on which to haul him down the stairs. I sat on the ground, driving my thumbs through my thick trousers, the spotted skin beneath, rubbing the prickling pain from my muscles, and as I fought nerve by nerve against the fingerling he bragged again about how he would one day take control, and that once he did my mind would be reduced to his former role, a prisoner pushed down, a belly-holed secret, wished forgotten. He would take my body and with it he would live his own life, in the house or on the dirt, among the trees of the woods or under the waters of the lake.

I had been given so many new bodies, he said, and one day he planned to rule them all.

MEMORY AS SADNESS DISCARDED, DENIED: To pretend to be unaffected by the almost-emptied rooms of the deep house. To pretend to have some other reasons to open again every door, scour every chamber, even after I knew what I would find, and so to lie to the fingerling, to claim I was looking for my wife, even though we both knew she was not there.

To claim to be hunting for the bear, even though as always she would find us, and not the other way around.

To be overcome at the tenth floor, then nearly emptied of reaction by the twentieth, and still to have a hundred more floors to walk, staircases to climb.

To eat what I could find, the cinders of the feast the foundling had claimed were always there, that I had not remembered, that I had believed poisoned, trapped as I would have trapped them.

To drink water fallen clean from the sky, now mixed black with what was once us, what were once the memories of my wife.

To again rub ashes into my face until my pores and ducts choked shut with my wife, so that I could not cry, so that my expressions were blanked by her absence.

And then in that state to reach the landing where my last descent had ended, that terminus jutted out from the last hall into the darkness surrounding, spread over the black that lay below, swirling around the spiral of the great stairs.

After the long walk trapped in the burned house there was some relief to again taste the better air of that wider chamber, but also some fear, because my failing eyesight could not penetrate the dark below or around, nor could my ringing ears locate the source of the cool wind that blew across the unbounded expanse. Rather than proceed immediately across the landing and onto the stairs, I stayed close to the last door of the deep house, lingered there until I believed myself ready. After some hesitation I approached the great stairs, and there I reached out my good foot to place it upon the first stair—and then I stumbled unbalanced upon my bad foot, nearly falling when I would not take that step—and how the fingerling laughed then, at my flaws again revealed.

The temperature dropped until I shivered constantly in my last clothes and in my tired bones, and then the fingerling lapsed quiet, his voice chilled, and so for a time he tormented me no more, let off his bragging, and rightly so: He had won much of what he'd stood to win, and what good had it done him? His rival the foundling was dead, and we were on our way to find his mother. And if she was dead too? Then even that might be no bother, as she was not the end of mothering, not even in this long-wearied world. Somewhere above or below there was the bear, hunting her way through the house, a danger, yes, but also another mother to whom the fingerling could be given, offered in replacement for her silenced cub—but then the bear was also more than one element, *bear* and *mother*, a combination we rarely spoke of, barely mentioned.

From below darkness leaked, and *black* too, had since before we first arrived at the landing, and soon the cold and the exhaustion of my long descent overwhelmed me, until there was no choice but to give more control to the fingerling, so that while I rested he might watch the stairs above. I instructed him to wake me at the first sign, and then I asked for his worthless promise, begged him to make no bargains of his own, for it was his mother he wanted, not this other who wanted his mother dead.

Before I slept I begged him to be no one else's foundling, and in the last moment of wakefulness I knew my mistake, how I had said too much: He had never before considered that there was more than one way to find a mother, more than one route to becoming a son, and now he said, WHAT IS THE DIFFERENCE BETWEEN A CUB AND A BOY?

He said, WHAT IS THE DIFFERENCE TO ME?

BUT LATER THE FINGERLING DID cry me from my sleep, as he spoke loud in all his many voices, each new tongue battering me up into wakefulness. How long had I slept? Long enough that my first movements caused my beard to spill nested spiders down my chest, their pale bodies scurrying across and into my clothes, and as I shook them from those folds, my sight cataracted, firing white points across the dark of the landing, and from too close the bear roared so that I hurried to push muscles against my rusty joints, made them to lift me from the ground, to point my beggar's bones in the direction of her approach. At my feet lay her shrouded son, smaller now, the sad shell of a departed ghost, and there would be no hiding his shape. I wet my throat with swallowed spit, and when the bear appeared — that bony armor, gathered across that muscled hump; that yellow mouth, set slavering in that wide-wedged head — even before she was fully emerged from the stairwell I began to speak, as fast and loud as I could.

With dream still slipping from my syllables, I said to the bear, My wife's songs have torn down the sky, have dug this deep house, have thrown moons up and dragged stars down, and I know you know these powers and of others besides.

I said, I know that you were once mighty too, but my wife has another song, one with the power to do what your music cannot. With this song my wife can restore your child, can find and bind the ghost of your cub to this boy, and then make him again into the bear he was always meant by you to be.

This is why I seek her, why I have waited here for you, where you might help me reach her.

I said, I know you killed your cub, shaped into our shape, and I know your misery must be absolute — absolute as your anger has always been.

I said, I do not know why you did it, but with my wife's help it can be *undone*.

I said these things, and then the bear roared, the force staggering me, and as she started her approach I spoke faster, finished what few words I had left to say — and I am sorry to say I said them — that when the bear's son was made whole again, then I would end my wife, as long ago I promised the bear I would.

I said, In return, you will make me be a bear too. You will breathe fur upon my skin and upon the skin of your son.

I said, We will be a family of bears, and you shall be its head forever.

But bears take no mates, marry no one. What children they have, they belong to mothers alone, and how little mother there was left to receive my words, the words I hoped were like those she wanted to hear, if there even were such words: Her bones remained long and thicker than ever, but as I had seen from the lake there was no fur atop her face or shoulders or flanks, barely even flesh where fur should have been. If her claws had pulled from her paws then it hardly mattered, because covering her everywhere were sharp points, spurs of bone come to replace those previous implements. Her eyes spun wide in the hollows of their orbits, and she seemed able to fix me only with one pupil or the other, never both at once, and while her wounded gaze shook me, it did not make me move my own hurt face away. Despite the rank rot of her speech, I stood fast before her, and as I watched the muscles move atop her murdering face I put between us another truth so that I might armor my lie within it: Before the falling of the moon, I said, I had been dead upon the floor of our house, heart stopped, and the foundling had sung me back into life — and this the bear did not want to hear.

The bear covered the last distance between us in a bound, knocking me to the stones with the slap of an uncurling fist. The foundling's shrouded body was beneath her and between us, and she stepped carefully around it even as she pressed the weight of her paw upon my chest. My ribs strained, and for a time my breath fled, and with wheezing growls she berated my deceptions, my dishonest intentions in all the moments from the first we shared upon the dirt until this one. Still I persisted in my story, kept to what had happened: I had been dead, and the foundling had given me life.

In the woods I had buried so many animals, and while I had seen what later fled up and out of their graves, I knew that what the bear had to offer was not new life but only some portion of the old come back, a portion subtracted from a better whole and never to be fixed again. And so I convinced her that the founding had learned this trick from his other mother, my wife, that there was a song that brought the human dead back to life, and only my wife and her foundling knew it. Not me, with my tone-deaf ears, and not the bear, with her language of barks and growls. Only working together would we see my wife again, and only together would we each get what we wanted.

The bear roared, and in her roar she said, All our pacts have been nullified, revoked.

After my cub is restored to me, then I will kill the thief for what she took from me, for what that taking cost.

After your wife is dead, then I will take my new cub and return to the woods, the woods that will grow where my woods once grew.

You I do not want. You will leave this place forever, returning to the country across the lake, and if ever I smell your scent again I will separate it from your skin with every tooth and claw I have left.

She said, I did not mean to kill my cub, but in the darkness and the fire his shadow grew long, and when I saw its length spread across the wall of my cave then I mistook him for you, clothed as he was in your stinking clothes.

THE BEAR LOWERED HERSELF BEFORE me, all her remainder shaking with the containment of her rage. I struggled aboard her broad shoulders with the foundling clutched to my chest, and the bear's armor cut my thighs as I tried to find some right place to saddle myself, and so each movement made a wound, and each wound itched and burned, and the burning bled the last sleep out of my legs, the body above.

The fingerling argued against my revealed plan, claiming that what had been impossible was made easy: Now there was a gap in the bear's armor between its head and its torso, a space where two plates of bone ground with each step, where my blade might slip between to spill her out, no longer having to saw through the layers of hair and skin and fat that once blocked entrance to the bear's jugular, its carotid.

The fingerling said, THIS TRUCE I CANNOT ALLOW, but by then it was too late, and the bear started down the great stairs with switchbacked bounds, plummeting from left to right of the fast-dropping spiral, and with my free hand I clutched at the sharp points of her shoulder blades, cried out as each leap cut me deeper, sawed at what little flesh was left.

The bear moved fast, and yet we seemed barely to advance, there being so many stairs above us, so many still dropping below. She leaped down the high and uneven steps, and while often she landed sure of foot she also sometimes stumbled, sliding sideways across the precarious stone of the steps. More than once I was nearly thrown from her shoulders, and each near fall left me shaken, clutching tight to all I needed to hold. At this depth, the walls around the stairs faded, and then sight and scent began to do the same, and even without the whole of those senses I perceived or believed I did that we were in a wide cave or carved chamber, farther bounded than any I'd experienced before. If there was sound at the edges of that space, then it did not reach us upon the stairs, and nothing flapped or flew or dripped through the yawning dark. Emptied of activity, the air thinned, and as we descended farther there was for a time only the bear's footsteps, her harsh breathing, and also my own constant wheezing, some effect of age or injury I could no longer suppress, each of our base noises flatter without the possibility for resonance or echo.

As she navigated the great stairs, the bear's growls of recognition turned again to speech and then to story, her heavy voice a tiring whisper, and through the fingerling she was translated and amplified, as she offered some last words into the grayer air where words could still be spoken.

The bear said, I do not know what you and your wife fled, but in my old country I no longer had any husband of my own. We had married and he had built a house, and then that house had burned, and then he had died in the fire, taking everything of him with him, and I had not even a child to remind me of him, only some wide scars of the burns I had suffered when I failed to save him, marks of what for some time I wished had consumed me too.

She said, Afterward I came to the dirt, but I did not build a house, did not know how, did not even want a house again, when houses had for me proved so temporary.

She said, From the first I lived in the cave, and in the day I walked the woods, picked its berries and dug its tubers, made for myself some simple life in which I owned nothing, in which I wanted for no other.

But there was already another here, she said, and he watched me, and later I felt him watching.

When I walked across the dirt, and then into the lake to wash myself and to swim in the cold gray water, there I found him waiting, and after he hushed away my reluctance he showed me many sights, both the surface of things and also what lay deeper beneath.

She said, It was he who showed me the black and also how to dive below it, first with him and then on my own.

It was there in the black that I changed for the first time, that I became some other shape than grieving woman, than widow bereft.

She said, I was not always a bear, but I was not before that just one other thing.

Neither was he, she said. He was both whale and squid, and once a man, once many men, perhaps.

He was so old when I met him, she said, but even in his old awfulness he could still be gentle, and in the lake-black our shapes did not matter, and so we were as one for a time, and the next time we separated I was two, one floating inside the other, and he was still his same multitude, his legion of possibility, a thousand shapes all wanting only to be made more, to be taken out of the lake and onto the dirt, then back into the other world, the country where what he was might spread.

All I wanted was one child, one boy to love, to take the place of the man I had lost, and when I saw I could not have just that then I hid his child inside me and refused all others, and with what strength he had taught me I kept him away until I could escape the black, the water above. Against his anger, I left the lake and went back to the woods, where I was sure he could not follow, and in my cave, among the dark shadows gathered between the world's broad bones, there I saw that it was our children who gave us shape, as much as we shaped them, and for my coming child I became a bear, meant us both be bears forever, so that what human miseries I had known might never know him.

The light from the fires above had long faded, and the broken shafts of light falling from the surface could not reach this deep either, and now there was only darkness. Or rather, not darkness but the whole of that element that I had never experienced upon the dirt, with its moon and its moons, and only partially under the lake. Now here was the fullness of the *black*, the truth of that element undiluted and worse than I'd imagined. The black was thick in places and hot too, and also it was cold and thin at other depths, and whatever it was it was always there. Other senses failed too, so that sometimes I could not feel my skin, goosefleshed with chill or else sweating and bloody, nor could I any longer hear through the weight of the black's silence. My tongue went numb, and the inside of my nose felt so full of silt that I could not clear it, and still the bear moved downward, still she bellowed soundlessly, as I felt her lungs fill and empty below my legs, when I felt anything at all.

Downward and downward she took us, navigating by something I could not sense, perhaps the smell of her cub's last disguised passing, perhaps the scent of the woman who stole him away. I could not even see my fingers in front of my face, but I felt or else imagined that the way occasionally flattened, straightened, that we arrived at wide landings, at whole floors riddled with black passageways leading away from the stairs toward other black chambers. It was only there among those widest floors that the bear became confused, almost lost. There she had to put her bloody nose to the ground and sniff for her trail, and I wondered how much better even her weakened senses were that she could smell so much through the black when I could not, and if what confused her was not losing the trail but rather having it fracture, spreading in too many directions, for even though those passageways were as yet unlit they were not empty, and if they were like those above, then they might have held me, might have held my wife, and also the bear and the squid and the fingerling and the foundling, and I saw in the bear's nosing of the stone floors that whereas the deep house had been mostly our past this deeper house could have been our future — but then that future was dark and cold, an emptied gulf where there was nothing to hear but silence, nothing to see but absence, nothing to own but our lack.

And then for some long span there was no light above and no light below, and no other senses either, and for a time no thought, only the black, the black and also us turning inward upon the stairs inside it, except for when I thought I saw what was once a star fall off in the distance, tunneling white-blazing through the senseless void, but surely I imagined the sights its light showed me, nightmares indescribable; and then even that blackest black, it could not go on forever, and although I did not mark when we began to emerge any more than I was sure when we had become fully immersed, there next came a returning of sensation, and with each step we descended, the black receded or was at last pushed back.

ONCE AGAIN I RECOGNIZED A graying of the air, some shelves of rocks jutting into sight, some cave walls closing in, and soon all these surfaces resolved into sight, wet with the moisture trapped under the earth, and that water dripped onto my face and my hands, waking my body from its stasis, the senseless sleep of our descent. Now there was no more hibernation, only a thousand small and vulgar pains: My thighs ached with the movement of the bear's bony plates, and my teeth shook in their sockets as I tested them with my tongue, that stiff organ suddenly dry and aching. I lifted my face, opened my mouth to let the moisture drip into me, each drop cooling some tiny fraction of the sore heat in my throat, and with light returning it was easier to see how blind I was going, had gone, how my one bad eye had become two. Soon I would see nothing at all, and I began to worry that I would arrive too late, that in her chambers I would not be able to look upon the wife I had come so far to find.

We were again upon a structure recognizable as a staircase, with a ceiling and a floor and walls close and closing in. Now there was the darker black above us and a lighter light below, and I felt my heart race forward, accelerating to let a rare bit of excited blood pass through its clogged valves and pumps, that fist of red muscle shaking anew, thudding my bones, setting their chorus to vibrating, and from inside that feeling I said, Hurry, I said, Hurry to the bottom now —

At the sound of my voice, the bear slipped, staggered, the front of her body lower than the back and now sliding sideways, and as I tightened my grip on the pommel of a protruding shoulder blade, the bone shattered, became a handful of dust. The bear cried out, bent the wide wedge of her head back upon me, and she was near blind then too, one eye clouded, the long-drooping other caked with layered rheum and salt, grinding as it turned in its orbit. She opened her mouth to make some warning, but there was so little growl left in her, too little to waste. Snot dripped from her caved nostrils, and the remains of her lips drooled white clumps of thirsty spit, and the cords in her neck jumped between her bones, so that I could see her stretched muscles working her toothless face, that countenance no less fearsome for its lack of skin, of underlying blood with which to make its hate known, and to that face I said, I am sorry.

I am sorry, I said.

I said, I am sorry, but still I must ask you to hurry.

How the bear hated me then, as I hated her: She stiffened beneath her bones, cast that hate's heat through what shell she had left, and then again we were descending, and as our pace resumed and then exceeded its prior state, the fingerling pulsed in my belly, grew bold against my touch. How much of my territory he had acquired, and now he returned to me only what I did not want, some other sensations I had set aside: My liver throbbed with him, as did my lungs, my gall bladder, the bone in my thigh. In my stomach was the worst pain, the first of it ever and now still there, fibrous and hard. I poked at that first tumor with my fingers, pushed him floating through the nausea, then gasped at the new pains in my bowels and in my balls, at the bloating that followed the fingerling's bulging against the walls of my organs, the inside of my abraded flesh, my hollowed skin.

The bear's body tensed beneath her armor, bristled the plates of bones around her head to quivering, and though the fingerling and I joined in her agitation still I did not see what the bear saw.

The memory of our arrival at the foot of the world, at the bottom of everything: To reach the ending of the staircase to find a wall and in that wall a door, inset into the stone.

To climb off the bear, holding the shrouded foundling against one shoulder so that my other hand might be free.

To stand back as the bear threw herself upon the door, knocking her claw-bones against its locked strength.

To let her roar herself empty, then to unfasten the stained join of my shirt, pull free my secret: the key to our house, the key that had forever fit all the doors of my wife's deep house, whenever I'd found them locked against me.

Then to put my palm against the cold stone of the door.

Then to push it wide and also to step through.

Then at last to understand: It was not a chamber my wife had built at the bottom of the great stairs but a house.

A house, and also a dirt, and also a lake, and also a woods.

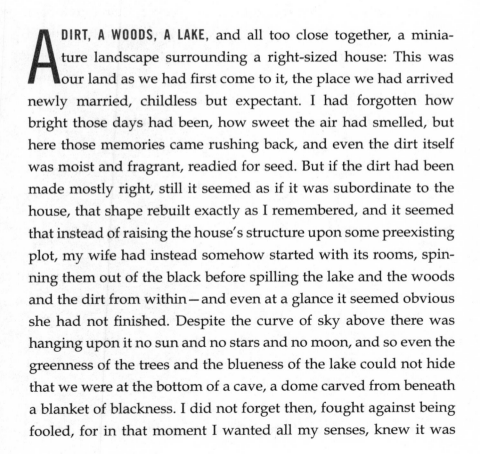

A DIRT, A WOODS, A LAKE, and all too close together, a miniature landscape surrounding a right-sized house: This was our land as we had first come to it, the place we had arrived newly married, childless but expectant. I had forgotten how bright those days had been, how sweet the air had smelled, but here those memories came rushing back, and even the dirt itself was moist and fragrant, readied for seed. But if the dirt had been made mostly right, still it seemed as if it was subordinate to the house, that shape rebuilt exactly as I remembered, and it seemed that instead of raising the house's structure upon some preexisting plot, my wife had instead somehow started with its rooms, spinning them out of the black before spilling the lake and the woods and the dirt from within—and even at a glance it seemed obvious she had not finished. Despite the curve of sky above there was hanging upon it no sun and no stars and no moon, and so even the greenness of the trees and the blueness of the lake could not hide that we were at the bottom of a cave, a dome carved from beneath a blanket of blackness. I did not forget then, fought against being fooled, for in that moment I wanted all my senses, knew it was important that I not succumb to this illusion, and so I observed only what original elements I recognized, and also some of their smaller parts: In the window of my wife's house there flickered the faintness of a gas-lamp, one nearly exhausted of fuel, and I thrilled at the sight, for I believed it meant she lived, that someone still lived inside her house.

The bear bellowed, shoved past me as I stepped farther out onto the dirt, her movements hurried with anger. I let her pass, and with the foundling left behind me in the passageway my hands were freed to drag back my torn and filthy sleeve to reveal my long-stalled watch, that round face, that hovered hand no longer walking its circles. With my other sleeve I scrubbed at its clouded surface, then abandoned my cleaning to wind its stem, and as I did when I tested our family with the fish and the rabbits, I invented my own rules to cause what would happen next—and my new rule said it did not matter what time it was, only that there was again time—and so I wound and I wound, and then I held that mechanism until the bear was halfway between the door and the house, and then with a flinch I let its wheel unwind.

What gasps racked my body then, and also the body of the bear! All that had been slowed now accelerated upon us, old inertias shuddering us forward until the bear's legs ran too fast, tripping each other, her bone knees smacking against swelled feet. She stumbled and fell forward into the dirt, her head tucked for protection from the crash, her momentum threatening to flip her bulk, but as her shoulders hit the dirt they caught, carved a furrow into the ground, a trench diagonal across the path to the house.

By the time I had gathered the shrouded foundling into my arms and stepped back through the door onto the last dirt, by then the bear was already up again, climbed free and turned back, her bone-limited expression impossible to read at that distance. And then fragments of that bone flying loose as she shook her body, freeing the dirt from her shell. And then snot and spit and bloody worse roping out from her mouth, out of other holes, wounds, opening sores. And then with each step, more dissolution, more disintegration of what shape she had held for so long—and as her body shattered all around her, perhaps she did understand what had happened, or perhaps not.

It did not matter, not then, not to me.

The bear hesitated for some moment, rolled her gaze between me and the still-unopened house, as I stepped forward with my wife's son held again against me, close in my care. She righted her stance, then proceeded to the house, where with her new paws she battered it as she had thrashed the logs of our first home. Here it seemed the bear held no power over the seams of the house, nor the strength of its walls, and her blows had no effect besides their terrible booming racket, echoed throughout the large chamber. The bear roared, her voice senseless with frustration, even if diminished, and I saw how in her anger she became more an animal, dumber and more dangerous, and while she worked her toothless jaws against my wife's unencroachable doorjamb I went another way.

Let the bear try for the house, I said. She will gain no entry, and follow us instead.

How sure I meant to speak, but how worried I might have sounded, and more so when I felt the fingerling's smirking shapes, all moving, all growing faster, radiating from my stomach and everywhere else: He was in my throat and in my spleen, in my liver and in the cork of my bones and flush throughout my head, so that my skull felt too full, so that all my thoughts were pressed in upon. I had not long left before he had the whole of me, but with that time I believed I could at least reach the lake. With every step its water pulled me more, its shimmer tugging at the shape that awaited within or else just outside my shell, an aura ready to be made flesh.

To have my breath stolen away. To stumble, one knee kissing the dirt. To stand and to struggle forward, and then to feel my voice lifted out of my throat and into the air, loud as my dry mouth allowed, and with it came the words the fingerling had waited so long to say, loud betrayals flung back toward the bear, her thrashing at the sound structure of the house:

SAVE ME, the fingerling said. SAVE ME INSTEAD OF YOUR CUB, AND I WILL NEVER LEAVE YOU.

I WILL NEVER DIE, he said. I WILL NEVER AGE.

I AM A CHILD WHO IS A GHOST WHO IS A CANCER AND I AM FOREVER.

I CAN KEEP YOU STRONG, AS I HAVE KEPT THIS WEAKEST MAN, AND TOGETHER WE WILL HAVE ALL THE LAKE AND DIRT AND WOODS WE WANT.

The fingerling said, KILL MY FATHER AND EAT HIS BODY, AND WITHIN HIM, YOU WILL FIND ME WAITING.

The fingerling said, HURRY, FOR HE IS ALMOST INTO THE WATER, and then the bear cracked the air with her anger, turned inside the sound of her voice. She bounded across the dirt, in pursuit of my burdened limping, and while I could have ensured my escape by casting aside the foundling I was unwilling to create an impasse where I held the lake and the bear held the shore—and then in only a few steps I was at the water's edge—and there the bear struck me just once, a terrible blow landed in haste, at the shallow threshold of the water and the land, the dirt and the lake.

THE BEAR'S FIST OF BONE struck me from shoulder to hip, through my back, scraped against skin and muscle and organ and rib, and by its force I was dropped into the water, the foundling still held tight against my chest, and as I fell I tucked him within my motion, curled his dead body in the curve of my still living one, and then in the shallows came the shift, the slide sideways into another shape so that I was no longer who I had been, or else I was still him and also something more, and then from behind me came the splashing of the bear following me out into the water, into the waves that spilled up to and then crested over her heavy head.

My next transformation was not about a mouth that became a beak, was not merely arms and legs that became tentacles thickened with hooks and suckers. Even the eyes of squid were not pathed as the eyes of men, and so new-sighted mechanisms had to be made in this instant, a second long enough. I was adept now at making do with what time there was, and so here there was time enough for one last plan, the quick purposing of my new body, the filling of it with its task: to kill this bear, this mother I pitied but whom the rules of this world would not let me save; who had frustrated me for so long; who had tried to kill me and had killed the foundling instead; whom I too had hurt, but whose forgiveness I could not earn.

And what was the fingerling's role in this fight, and whose side would he take?

Perhaps he had imagined he would be able to again frustrate me, but now it was I who frustrated him, with a body made strange, its hollows unfamiliar tunnels: If he lived part of his life in my spleen, where would he go now that I had no spleen? Where were my new lungs, my new gall bladder, my new arms and legs? For the fingerling, who had besieged my bones to bending, where was there to go when I had no bones?

Only one place, a chamber clenched.

The squid had reshaped my body but it was not all a part of me, and so I too was a passenger or else a pilot, as the fingerling had been between my bones, and while the squid first jetted toward the center of the lake, away from the bear, it soon began the long arc back, by my command. The bear was still bellowing through the shallows when we struck her the first time, raking a hooked tentacle from out the water and across her bony trap-scarred snout, and she howled in pain or frustration. The squid pressed, circled, pressed again, put our hooked and barbed tentacles to their use, all our arms with more reach than even the bear's own long grasp, and also with a beak the equal of her mouth, if not its better, the bear's now loose of tooth and weak of jaw, but still the squid did not bring our full fight upon her, not while she was able to stand in the low water. Instead we pulled and tore her flesh, her facing flank, and with quick blows we lured her on, and when she began to falter and to wail only then did we taunt her failing courage with the shrouded shape of her once-cub, the foundling pushed out into the lake, floating bloated upon the surface and waiting to be claimed.

How the bear bellowed then! Grayest water shook from off her roaring head, her bone mantle glistening in the false light sparkling all the surface of my wife's new-sung world, and then the bear charged into the deeper water, fast again, fast as she had moved between the trees of her own woods. When her feet left the lake floor, without hesitation she swam on, her armored legs pumping beneath the water, churning her path as she struggled to keep her snout above the surface, pointed at the floating shroud still out of reach. The water was deep and cold, deeper and colder than its small circumference suggested, and into those depths the squid dove, and from those depths we rose again to strike at the bear, to rake our hooks across her belly, the bones of her armor, and despite those gouges we could do no real harm, would never except in that space the fingerling had shown me, that bone-bare stretch of her throat that we could not yet reach. As the bear swam, the squid frustrated her with our speed, with our ability to attack then quickly retreat, moving from her floundering shape to the floating body of the foundling, and there was no danger to me then, so deep inside: From this new station I was never once afraid of the bear, as I had been on the dirt and in the woods and in the house. All my years upon the dirt the bear had seemed to master me, and now I would master her.

As we fought, the fingerling moved within the corridors of the squid shape, assuming new posts and positions, and as the squid swam around the bear so also the fingerling was set in motion inside that movement, testing every space. The fingerling approached an organ much like the stomach he had claimed, and when he was wormed deep inside that clenched and puckered sac, then at my command the squid charged up through the depths toward the struggling bear, and there I said goodbye, goodbye to son and ghost, goodbye to bear and other-mother, other-wife who was never mine, and if they did not wholly deserve this end they got, at least they were ended, and what mercy I believed that was: To steer the squid to swim before the bear, leading her on, then to turn our body back. To feel the squid release into the water the contents of our ink sac like a fist opening, the unfolding of a hand holding some smoky darkness, holding blackness, my blackness, yes, all that ghost I had named the fingerling when it deserved no other name, and now that son, caught there in that organ, and now that son expelled at last, swimming out into obfuscation, into a cloud of camouflage, into a cloud of grief through which the squid swam, my past floating outside our body, and still I felt nothing, still I saw with the dispassionate yellow gaze of the squid — or else how could I have done what I did — and the voice and the voices of my only son surrounded us, made a cloud that was not just ink, and in it the squid saw everything and the bear saw nothing, and the water churned with the stuff of our ink and the unmakings of the fingerling, torn and threaded by the sharp slimness of that expelling orifice, and as this animated ink he floated in streaks and flumes around the bear, whose mouth filled when she growled to smell him, the clotted stink of something rotten unbirthed, gestated too long.

The squid was a hunter and a trapper too, and I was the squid, and the squid was me, and we shot through the ink toward the bear, searching for that thin breadth of bone-spaced chance, and as we jetted through that horror I heard the fingerling's voice call out to me, call out in many voices for me to save him, to take him back in, begging as only a child can beg. Despite his treacheries he was sometimes somehow still a baby boy, and had I been a man his drowning might have undone the taut strings with which I had shut my heart.

As a squid?

As a squid I saw only a food we would not eat, flesh of my flesh, poison if I made the same mistake again. His blackness streamed around us, but all the squid cared was how it hid our long shape, masked our sharp scent. We swam the wet length of our clouded boy, and when the squid reached the bear we sought again to strike her where she needed to be struck, and against us and against the fingerling the bear struggled to surface, her mouth and eyes and ears filling with the bodies of my son, with the minnowed shapes of him. And what shapes they were! Not just ink and boy but already hunger and hatred clumping, solidifying, becoming new shapes, new forms of ancient and angry swimmers, each frustrating the bear, then tearing at her eyes, then dismantling the last solid sockets of her jaw, then eating her tongue from out her mouth.

Soon the bear was blind and belligerent, confused so that she did not know up or down, and the squid circled her flailing once, twice, amid the ink. I wanted to speak to her, to reach out and say some parting words — to say *sorry, sorry* again — but the squid did not have the same brain as a man, nor the same vocal cords, and without the fingerling I could not have translated her replies, and anyway what right words were there to say.

The squid dragged our hooks across the bear's stomach, this time breaking her weakened bones across new perforations, leaving furrows for the black ghosts of the fingerling to crack wider, and when that succeeded we laid down more cuts, across the hump of the shoulders and both halves of the hips, across the plates of the bear's back and head. I needed the squid to strike the throat, craved that hit, but could not help my marveling at our thoroughness, the glory of this hunter's shape, so different from my trapper's form upon the land, for the squid was an exquisite killing machine and within it I an exquisite killer. The ghosts of the fingerling hungered, desperate outside my strong-shelled body, and with no other source in the empty lake they redoubled their attack on the bear, tore strings of marrow from out her bones, and with them they grew quickly larger, shaped more like fish, then more like eels. Black scaled and dark slimed, they wiggled in and out of the bear's armor, and when they slipped away it was with gulping throats, bloated stomachs.

All around me was the squid, and all around the squid was the black of our ink, my own personal black, a trap carried for so long so that it might snare the bear, so that within it the squid might drag her down, and I wondered then: Did she remember the first squid, in the lake above, how he too showed her the bottom of his lake? How there he promised her its future?

Did she realize that future had happened, and that here at last it was at its end, the last of the present, the beginning of the forever-past, and the bear was no human woman anymore, no bear-mother either, but some other thing, adversary made killer made legend: And although I might have felt remorse at the killing of a woman, how could I feel the same for a myth, this unlovable story?

We sensed only the slightest resistance as our hooks swung through the slice of space between the bear's head and neck, just a small snag and then another as those sharp edges dragged through the windpipe and the jugular and the carotid, and then the squid pushed forward, shoved our head into that space as another squid had entered into my chest, and with our beak we tore the bear until a loud rising of air filled the water, then pink foam, then black, and then and then and then, and then to be the squid and to have the squid be me, to together be a hunter who had hunted: to swim unflinched as the bear jerked inside our embrace, then to feel her loosen, limp out. And after we finished tearing loose her throat, then we released her bulk to swim arcing away, so that her unblubbered bones might slowly sink, burdened by the heavy weight of the many fingerlings, their shapes come hungry to feed.

WHAT ACCOMPANIED US THEN BUT a child's cacophony, the fingerling's voice not one speech but a thousand, a thousand thousands, all together the sound of a break, and of a fracture. I had given him an innumerable number of pains, and he had returned to me the same, and now all of those hurts would own the depths of this lake, would feed on the bear for as long as it took to take her inside their many mouths, and so at least he would possess the mother he had wished to possess, as much as I had possessed him.

As I swam, I wanted to call out to the fingerlings, all the many schools fluttering around. I wanted to speak to them, but not to give them commands, not fatherly warnings or threats or pleas or admonishments. At last I wished to offer only names, all the names we had meant to give our many children. I wanted to give the fingerling what he had long ago asked me for, but I had no human mouth and so could offer nothing more, and anyway it was nothing he gave me back, neither satisfaction nor forgiveness nor a surface on which to attach my sadness, my relief. Whatever forms the fingerling next took on, none would be my son, and not my wife's either. The fingerling had gone too far already, even though it had been only minutes since our separation, the annulment of our sharing the space within my shape. Now he had taken his leave of me and I of him, and whoever next heard his many voices would not be me.

The squid gathered the foundling in our two largest tentacles, our strongest arms, then in powerful spurts jetted us back to the shallows, where I could again stand, become the husband, and in my arms the foundling became the son, the only son. As I came out of the water I came out of the squid too, and as a man I smelled the foundling's death differently, took in the decay that had rushed forward from the restarting of the clock. Upon the shore was my satchel, its strap cut from my back by the bear's last blow, and as I gathered it up I smelled it too, the two bearskins within it. All felt foul and also fouled, and I could feel the wrongness of their long carryings, my keeping them from the grave or the pyre or the lake. I had brought these as offerings for my wife, but what good thing was I bringing?

A corpse and the coverings of corpses.

To the very end, I had always been the weakest one, and yet it was only I who had gone on and on. Among all the unfair worlds in which we lived, all the other elements had fallen and failed, and still there was me, still there was *husband*. Now here I was, arrived, alone—and always it was in my loneliness that I had best survived—and in the next moment the front door of the house opened, and from that portal out stepped my wife, but not the wife I had known.

I EMERGED FROM THE LAKE to see her standing in the doorway of her house, the house that was only hers, so much like the one that had been ours. My wife lingered half in and half out, her hands clenched against the doorframe, that bordered threshold between the dirt and the house, and as I jerked my body up the path I saw even at that distance how the muscles of her face made her mouth to move, but also how no words escaped. With the foundling in my arms, I hurried as best my ruin would allow, and as I walked I rang out her name, voiced it forth into the air, made the shape of its three letters, vowel and consonant and vowel again.

I called her as she was called, but she gave no sign that she heard, or that if she heard she recognized the name, and when I called again her only response was alarm, perhaps fear: at my presence, at the sight of the foundling and me together, pathed from the lake to the house. As I got closer, I saw she had been changed as I had been changed, not just by age but by some other circumstances too: Where once she had looked the part of a woman I had known, now she was fevered into some new person, a scorched wife. As the foundling had described, there had been a fire lit within her, and while it had not consumed her flesh it had filled her with its heat, so that she could wear no clothes, so that her pale skin was darkened like burned and crackled paper, and her hair was become white, robbed of its pigment. And no matter what I said, still my wife did not speak, still she did not say a single word.

This last memory of my long search, memory as failure, as failure, a faltering: To scream her name again. To kneel before her, and then to lay prostrate at her smoking feet. To thrust wildly at the air with her single syllable, that balanced word, that unanswered name savaged with disuse. To kneel, holding the foundling, rocking his shrouded shape, unable to make my wife accept what had been brought.

To want already for that moment to be over but to fear that afterward there would be only worse moments to come. And so to still be the husband and to be the father but to have neither role acknowledged and in this absence of expected station to want for time to stop again, but to know that clockless hours were gone for good.

U PON THE PORCH, ALL OF me dripped, gushed, my naked wounds made known before my transformed wife: The trap-crushed ankle throbbed again with the wrongness of its healing, and without the fingerling's support the bear-wrenched shoulder hung crooked from its socket, and while those old wounds cried first it was the most recent that spoke loudest. The blood from that wound streaked, streamed around the almost-aligned knuckles of my spine, over my gooseflesh and old scars. Damaged breath wheezed from between the small remnants of my teeth, and as I sucked more air to say her name again I dizzied, my vision all sparks.

I did not know what other words to say, and so I said her name, said it until I was emptied of its sound, and then when I was hoarse and breathless I breathed it back in, and all I wanted in return was for her to speak some part of what I had come so far to hear: my own name returned, perhaps, or else an accusation, best followed by the terms of my eventual forgiveness.

Only after I quieted myself did she crouch down beside me, sinking her knees into the pool of my leaking.

She took my face between her hot hands, and then holding my cheeks — and then the smell of singed beard, of steamed tears — and then holding me, she said, Who are you?

She said, Where have you come from?

She pointed to the foundling, shrouded in dirty white, and as her accusing gaze lingered she said, Who is this, and why have you brought him?

And then, as if she had not already broken me, she turned and stepped back across the threshold, shutting the door.

I waited upon the porch, listened at the wood of the house, strained for the clatter and clack of objects within. After some moments had passed the door reopened, and this woman who had been my wife stepped back out onto the porch, reached out a hand. I took her fingers, took too much of them, and weaved them into mine, and though her heat hurt me I did not recoil, had waited too long to pull away in pain. At her request, I left the foundling momentarily upon the slats of the porch, then followed her out onto the dirt, where each step of hers burned away even what few patches of grass there were, and then in a circle of dirt she stopped and turned back, surveyed my wounds, the many leaks and lacerations upon my body.

With her index finger, she counted each, and as she touched them her heat sizzled and then cauterized the wounds shut, until eventually all that was left would stay there, heavy within me.

Amid the pain and stink, again her voice, again saying, Who are you?

Saying, Where have you come from?

Saying, Whose shroud is that upon my porch?

I am your husband, I said.

You left me, I said. Because you had a son, and after you left I looked for you, and later you sent him to look for me —

I said, I am your husband, and you were my wife, and together we had a son.

I said, I promise you, you are my wife still.

She listened to me speak, and then she shook her head.

No, she said. Always I have been here, and always I have been alone. Almost always it has only been me, and no other.

We were naked together upon the dirt, but still we were not as one. When I tried to argue my case, she stopped me, put a finger to my mouth, burned a streak across my already-chapped lips.

Later, she said. I am so tired.

It is time for me to rest, she said, and then she dropped my hand and turned back for the house.

Where will I go? I asked. Where will I go next?

Then come, she said, and it was as easy as that, and then she said, It does not matter to me.

Without waiting she passed through the door and into the house, and then I lifted the foundling and carried him across that threshold, and also the satchel containing the two furs, the one real and one made. While my wife disappeared farther into the house, I returned to the entranceway to shut the door against the day-like light, the almost lack of wind outside. At last husband and wife and child were again gathered under one roof, and that alone was better than what other states had for so long persisted, on all the other floors of this world.

THE LAYOUT OF THE LAST house was the same as the one we'd shared, and in the front room, I saw a wood-framed sofa like one I had built and that she had upholstered with song, set again before a fireplace clean and piled beside with kindling. On the walls hung framed photographs of our wedding day, pictures that in our first house had been destroyed by the bear, and while my wife had forgotten everything, here everything was. With the spotted tips of my fingers I touched the image of my wife's face, and also mine, and that couple was long gone now, and it was no wonder she did not recognize us, and yet still there was something there, in or around the eyes, perhaps, or in the set of a mouth, the shape of a nose or neckline: a man and a woman just married, terrible in the potencies of their youth, their early love.

And in the kitchen: All our bowls as they had been when first stacked in their crates, before they were chipped and scratched by the bear's expulsion of our lives from her cave. All our spoons, shiny upon the wall. All our pots and pans, suspended from their hooks, hung above the hewn-wood counters, and in the pantry only shelves, surfaces bare because I was not there to hunt or to gather, because my wife hadn't the strength to harvest her garden — and so she had fed the foundling herself, herself nothing.

And in the dining room: A table set for two but with chairs enough for four. A candelabra with no candles. A layer of dust thick enough to hide the desire for family that once inhabited the room.

And in the nursery: The baby blankets my wife had sewn to show me she was trying. The bassinets I built to encourage her to produce what they might hold. The rocking chair I carved, the mobiles I strung. And because I did not know where else to lay the foundling, I brought him to lay upon that floor, in that room with no bed big enough to hold this slow-grown child. His shroud, ripped and dirty as it was, was still our wedding sheets, the once-white linens we were given, on which we tried our best to make our children, on which our losses slowly stained the white brown, no matter what soaps we scrubbed against its threads.

I walked down the house's single hallway, to the door at the end where our bedchamber once was. My wife had not yet emerged, and so I knocked, and when there was no answer I knocked again, and when there was still no answer I pushed the door open.

There I saw my wife collapsed on the floor, smoking the hardwood and gasping aloud, her skin dark and also alight, the opposite of my long-cold paleness, that mark of my late life spent below the earth. I did not have far to carry her, but as I lifted her she burned me wide, scorched the arms that held her, the chest that clutched her close. Then came the stench of more crisping hair, and afterward I wore some shirt of blisters, raised and swollen where they were not burst by the boiling. The pain was extraordinary and did not diminish as I swept aside the burned blankets to reveal a bed made of stone, a copy of the one we had shared but that had required no wood. I laid my wife down upon that slab—upon her side of the bed, the side on which she had always slept—and then I slumped upon the floor beside her, listened to the long syllables of nonsense accompanying the slow smoke that escaped her mouth.

After I could not wake her I carried buckets of water from the shallowest parts of the lake, whatever inlets I could reach without risking falling in, then returned to the house to soak some towels, found where our towels had always been. I laid each one across some surface of my wife's body, her forehead, her face and neck, her breasts and collarbones and belly and hips, her thighs and calves and feet—and each steamed, then smoked, then flamed — so that I had to snatch it back, burning my fingers. I was afraid to touch her, but when next she moaned I could not resist, and as I put my hand to her forehead to smooth back her hair, then that skin crinkled like ripping paper, and as always there was no good deed that did not worsen my crimes.

I could not sing as my wife could, and she would not wake no matter how I tried to cool her body with lake water or chilled air, let in through the now-open windows of the bedchamber, and because I did not know what else to do I again took her hand in mine, held on even as her heat opened my calluses, and as we burned together I began to speak, to tell her who she was, who she was to me.

I said, Remember I had finished building the house, or nearly so.

I said, Remember how terrible we must have seemed that day, when together we thought our marriage would then and always be celebrated.

I said, Remember: When we first arrived upon the dirt between the lake and the woods, then there was still sun and moon, only one moon, and stars too, all the intricacies of their intersections circumscribing the sky, their paths a tale to last every night, a waking dream to fill the hours of every day.

MEMORY OF MY WIFE'S CONFUSION, of her confused lack of memory: To know that she did not know who I was, even when she awoke in the middle of my story, in the middle of my telling her.

To understand she would not know her own name, no matter how many times I repeated it.

But as I spoke, her skin stopped smoking, lost some of its hottest heat even as it then stayed black and brittle. Encouraged by this cooling I confessed and confessed, and as the words moved out of my body and into the air, then with each story I saw her fever abate, diminished by right-ordered speech as it had not been by the wet cloths I had earlier tried. With each wrong-uttered word, each mistake I made or half-truth I told, the process reversed itself, set her body back toward ruin, and so I grew more careful, talked slower, put my tale on the surest path from our past to our present, smoothed out its digressions, its shifts of attention and time.

Soon I could touch the whole of her hand, then stroke her whitening forearm, and often she did not object to my touches, although if asked who I was she said she knew only whom I had claimed at great length to be. The blackness continued to leave the surface of her skin, revealing a face smooth and unwrinkled, unaged by memory, and while my speech tried to complicate that blankness, too often my words evoked no emotion.

It wasn't until I spoke of finding the furs in the deep house that I thought I saw some new reaction upon her face, a restrained titter, or else a twitch approximating surprise or recognition or grief, perhaps a new turn of the lips, a narrowing of the eyes. It was so slight I could not identify its exact character, but whatever it was I wanted more, and before I continued I went into the front room and retrieved my satchel, and from that satchel I took one of the cub-sized furs — their previous movements so calm now — and when I gave her that fur she squeezed it tight against her chest.

And again, my questions, my asking, Do you know yet who you are?

Do you know who I am?

Do you know why you're crying?

Still she shook her head, and still she denied, and her tears did not last long, not with her body still so hot. All the pieces of her I found in the deep house now went back into her, were returned by story, a different manner than they had escaped, sung into the rooms of the deep house: Now they came carried upon my breath, upon the word, these stories of dead child and dead bear and dead child, dying world.

After the story of the moonfall, I helped my wife from the bed, dressed her in some of the clothes hanging in her closet, as I had dressed myself earlier, in a shirt and trousers I had not seen since the youngest days of our marriage. Once she was clothed and shoed, then I had to sit down again, to gather myself before her, this ageless vision of the woman I had known and loved, long before our many complications, whom I was still growing used to in this new and unexpected shape.

And who was I to her, by the same light?

Still only a stranger, old and stooped, limping, long bearded and filthy.

She helped me down the hallway and into the front room, then out of the house, onto the porch, onto that fey-lit dirt. Her chamber's stale air circulated different than the air above, and at its first taste I began to cough, and then I could not stop coughing. My wife let go of my arm, the arm I'd meant to support her instead, and I doubled over, hacked and wheezed, but for a time no relief came. Afterward I looked up at her blank patience, and then I said, Do you remember yet? How to create shape and sense from a song? How to make a garden out of the dirt or moons out of the sky?

I said, Once, you made a boy out of a bear, and sometimes I look at you and I think you almost remember.

My wife did not respond, but I thought I saw some flicker of emotion move across her face, and then her hair again seemed to blaze behind her, or else it was only the wind and the weird light.

My wife, I said, and because I didn't know what else to do I stood to take her hand in mine, linked our fingers together. I set our feet upon the path that led from the house to the woods, the new and dark-barked trees, not as tall or broad as those found above but just as evenly spaced, and beneath them the pine straw was just as thick, lit by a similar diffusion of light. But here there were no badgers to be seen, no deer or elk, nor pheasants or quail, no sound but the wind, and there were no buck scrapes along the low trunks of the trees, no owl pellets coughed up and left for some scavenger. And there was likely then no cave, and this I believed

I knew even without checking, because when my wife made this place she perhaps did not remember that there was supposed to be a cave, a cave and also a bear.

While we walked, I told my wife of when I first reached the great stairs, but no matter how I described it she did not recognize this landmark, nor my name for it, and so I tried again to explain, tried to find a better way to teach her what she herself had made or else first discovered.

I told her about fighting the bear at the burying ground, and at last she traded silence for curiosity, asking me, But what is a bear?

Next I told her about the bear killing the whale or the squid, and she asked, What is a whale? What shape is a squid's?

And how to explain to someone who has never seen a bear what *bear* means, or *whale*, or *squid?*

What is the word *child*, even, if you have never seen a child?

She said, I wish—

She said, I would have liked to have had a husband, and I would like to have a son.

She said, It has been so lonely here, all by myself, as I have always been.

Maybe this house once belonged to someone else, she said, some other woman.

She said, Perhaps it was her you came looking for, but she is already gone. Perhaps I am someone else, and you are only mistaken in the way you look at me.

I said her name, begged it of her, said, Please, and then I said her name again.

I said, Do you remember any of the songs, the ones that might still save your boy, that could save me too, if there is enough of me left?

Please, I said. Please tell me that you do.

My wife, I let her go, or else she pulled loose, walked away, a step or two steps or three. She crossed and uncrossed her arms, then let them hang at her sides, hands open near her hips. She spread her legs just wide of her shoulders, opened her chest to fill it with air: a singer's stance, and how my heart moved to see it.

A breath, a deep breath, and then a deeper one: She sucked the strange air until she was filled, and then she looked into the non-sky, into the place where moon or stars would have hung if there had been moon and stars.

She looked up through the trees, and then with a turn of her mouth she released that air, that potentially song-held breath.

What then?

What else. Only something hard sounding, a bleat, a blather. Not just not a song but also not a melody, not a chord, not a single note.

She tried, then tried again, but each try was worse than what had come before, and there was nothing of who she was within her sound.

My wife said, I'm sorry.

She said, I wanted there to be a song, a song for you.

She said, I wanted to make you happy.

I nodded, knew. Again I took up her hand. I said, You must be so very tired.

I said, It's time for you to sleep.

I said, In the morning, we will bury our son.

I FOUND MY SHOVEL OR one like it in its accustomed spot, the place I once put it, the place some earlier, less-forgetful wife sung it back. Leaned against the rear of the house, it had shared space near the edge of the garden with my traps, but now there were no traps, and also nothing for them to catch, and that too was best.

And then back around the yard and onto the porch and inside the house, where my wife waited, where the shrouded foundling waited dumb in her arms.

And then outside again to hold the front door open so that my wife might carry her unremembered son out of our house, to lift him once more over the threshold and onto the dirt, and because I did not know where else to put him I buried him in the woods, in the same part of these new woods that I had claimed in the old, where I took the logs for our house, where I interred every beast I could. But all those days were gone, and I had promised this new woman whom I couldn't not call my wife that I would stop speaking of them, and the digging took all morning, as my wife could not work the shovel, and I was too sick for fast work. And so another element of our world was ended, and I believed for a time that no more would come.

I avoided my wife's blank gaze as I received the foundling's body from her, and then I lowered her son into his grave, and then I took the two furs from my satchel to blanket them across his shape—and when that first shovel weight of dirt hit heavy upon the shroud, it was only I who cried.

I **N THE WEEKS THAT FOLLOWED** I made my living again within the house, although I did not broach the borders of the marriage bed. Instead I took the crib and bassinet and rocking chair out onto the dirt, and in the yard I broke them, and then I made the nursery mine. Into it I gathered all the remaining artifacts of who we were, those same reminders that failed to stir my wife: the photographs of our wedding, the clothes we wore on our wedding day, still preserved, and also the gifts we had been given then, meant to start our life together. Emptied of those objects, the proper house became appropriately blank, and now those shapes that I could not discard would hurt me only in private, in the length of my sleepless, darkless nights.

There were no fish in the lake nor beasts in the woods, and so we ate from the small garden behind the house, where my wife's garden had always been, where perhaps some garden had always been meant to go. There were no pests to eat her crops—but also no bees to fertilize them, no worms to upturn the dirt, and no proper sun to light them—and so what grew there was also odd, plentiful but misshapen, underripe, without much flavor but nutritious enough. It was an unworkable garden, one whose half-sung mechanism would eventually fail from incompleteness, and when I asked her where she found her first seeds, she said that she did not know, that the garden had always grown exactly this well.

I said, Did you forget, or did you never know?

I said, How long ago did you start to forget? Do you at least know that?

She knew so little, despite my long storytelling, and when despite my promises I again reminded her that once she was able to make this whole world we now lived in, had somehow carved it free from the black, then she shook her head, said it was I who was mistaken.

She said, Why would I make a world so unfinished, if I were making it for me? Do you think I adore emptiness, or else a creation incomplete? When you speak of a bird, its wings, its feathers, I think to myself, That is something I would like to see. When you tell me of the bear, I wonder what its fur felt like under your hands and how its spoor smelled and how terribly frightening its roar must have been, even before it was the broken thing I saw from my window. And these fish you speak of, sparkling silver, why would I not want to feel their swimming around my ankles, the smallest minnows nipping at my toes, as if it were they who were meant to eat me, instead of the other way around?

I said, Once you did know.

I said, It was you who made this place.

My wife shook her head again, touched my face with her now-cool fingers. She said, How do you know these things about me? How do you pretend to know?

I said, Once you brought your son here to escape me, but there couldn't have been this world, waiting. This is a remaking of the world we shared, the only world your son had ever known.

I said, You tried to make him a home, and for some time you succeeded.

My wife again wanted to speak, but first she stared off into the twilit sky, the dark-that-was-not-dark of our morning. She was again so beautiful, her grace terrible in equal proportion to her sadness, and after she gathered herself she said, No, this world has always been here. I did not make it. Always it was here, waiting for me to find my way.

She said, I have listened to your story and I have been moved by your words, but I do not believe you are my husband, that the boy we buried was my son.

And then I knew I should have shown her the foundling's face, what was left of his face, how her song had made his into hers, had claimed even his nose and mouth and eyes, made them as hers were made, adopting him not just in claim but also in shape, and had I proved the foundling I would have proved it all.

My wife listened to my words, considered my trembling insistence, then said, It would not have mattered.

She said, While you slept, I opened his shroud myself and saw nothing like what you say I should have seen. Just a dead boy, whose death meant nothing to me.

Every day after I woke up to the same old touches, mindless now but still hot and cold, thick and thin, beneath and atop my skin. I coughed, spit up into the bucket I had left there for just this purpose, and when I was finished I took the bucket outside and limped it down the path to the lake, where I dumped its runny contents into the waters. There tiny black fish swam into the shallows to eat this bloody vomit, and I did not tell my wife I recognized them but rather kept their existence to myself.

A new secret then, but even if I had told her, would she have understood? Could she have looked into the water to see that the slim length her body aborted was become a school of fish or something like fish, as hungry for their father's flesh now as when they were younger and meant to be a boy?

And so I said nothing. And so I continued to say nothing, even as other signs began to reappear, recur: Because I was sick I could rarely stand more than a few bites of what we gathered from the garden, and after each such meal, my wife asked me why I did not eat, and when I did not answer, she asked what she had done wrong in the kitchen. I hurt her anew as she asked again every evening, my mere presence enough to reintroduce doubt, my voice and my actions or lack of action enough to allow the reentry of guilt, that emotion I had carried from the top of the world to its very bottom, where now it pooled and stained all that I touched, all those I longed to touch, and it was after the frustrations of one of these late meals that we first heard the voices, the high laughter from within the woods, cut through the stillness of the dimming light, the unbroken content of our evening.

I did not hear before my wife heard, did not hear until after she asked me and asked me again if I did, but then afterward what withered flesh that sound made, my skin pebbled along every nerve line, the shivers of recognition jerking me from my chair. Together my wife and I rushed toward the woods, but she arrived there faster, possessed of a new youth, her body restored as fully as her mind was not. From farther ahead her voice called out for me to hurry, and although I wanted to respond, all that breath was already engaged in moving my bones toward her and the voices beyond, and any speech I would have made would not delay the process, and then anyway I was soon enough arriving, looking up from watching my feet to spy my wife, tall and pale and stunned, some short distance across the tree line, and there to see how she was surrounded: by the foundling, by a new crowd of foundlings.

T THE EDGE OF THE woods stood some small number of sons, all so similar at first but marked apart the more I looked. The foundlings were all their own ages, for one thing, and each carried a slightly shifted face upon its head, a different expression of lips and mouth and teeth. Their appearance put my heart to pounding but did not disturb my wife, who already knelt before their approach, bidding them to come to her, inviting their hands upon her face and body. She gathered these boys close, took some into her arms, and there I saw a mockery of the family I had wanted, some clutch of children encircling this one woman, this woman I had always wanted above all others, and my face twisted as I saw a seventh son wandering out of the thicker brambles, stumbling with his face struck wide across the forehead—as if bleeding from the blow of a boat, as if struck hull across head—impossibly saying MOTHER, saying MOTHER wetly, with lungs soaked and sodden from a lake, and again he said MOTHER, MOTHER, and then all that water inside followed his voice out, spilling onto the forest floor, soaking his words into its soil.

Confronted with this dying child, my wife did not scream, did not even glance in my direction, while some short distance away this staved foundling fell, his voice no longer capable of words, and the other children seemed as undisturbed as my wife. They did not speak well—the true foundling had never fully outgrown the stutter and stammer of his childhood—but that did not stop them from leaving my wife to come to me, to put their cold hands upon my face, and with their different lisps they said SHHH, they said DON'T WORRY, they said MOTHER WILL BRING HIM BACK, and then there were more of them coming, walking out of the woods, and when they came they came dressed as these first were dressed, all in white, each garment featureless from a distance, but close up embroidered with pale stitching on pale cloth, the markings of our wedding sheets.

My wife stood among the growing crowd of children, all of them coming to her, and from their midst she said to me, What are we supposed to do?

She said, Are we supposed to take care of these children, and what does that mean?

As if I knew. As if there were any laws that had proved constant, reliable. And so I said nothing, because I did not know, because part of me did not want to find out, did not want to commit to another fruitless course of action, whether that was caring for these foundlings, these children found by both of us, whether it was refusing to do so. I was not as convinced as my wife that these foundlings were anything we should lead out of the woods and onto the dirt, and I did not hide my gladness when we found we could not: My wife gathered the children into a single-file column, and in this formation they followed her eagerly until the tree line—but there they would follow her no more, their fear of that threshold seemingly the exact opposite of the first foundling's, who had for many years refused to return to the woods.

My wife abandoned her garden after the coming of the foundlings, let its plants grow wild again, as perhaps they had before. I followed her lead, went with her into the woods each morning and afternoon to watch the foundlings, and every day there were more among the trees, and always my wife tried to gather some to her, as many as she could. None came with names, and she remembered no such sounds to grant them, to mark this one from that one further than their shifted features already had, and while there were many such names within me, saved for the children we never had, I decided I would not give them to her, no matter how she pleaded.

Despite the evidence of their play, I said these were not real children, that I preferred them nameless, as even if they were real I did not believe they would prove permanent. So few things had, and I wished to never again love what would not last, and while my wife delighted in the company of these children, I did not.

In the deep house there had been a room for every aspect of my wife's person, and here there was a foundling for every aspect of her son's, and among them were those that reminded me most of that child we raised together: One foundling, five or six years old, gathered some of the younger ones into a circle, then thrilled them with stories previously captured in our stars, stories about the elements my wife had taught to our own foundling, all that old trap of *house* and *dirt* and *moon* and *ghost*. I listened long to his explanations, but he did not say *mother*, did not say *father*, and so either we were now unnecessary or else he was only some anomaly too, some slightly false son, and somewhere there would be a foundling who knew all the elements, and also their order. Elsewhere, another son knew none of our elements, and so named *rock* and *stream*, *dust* and *dream*, and also there were others who subscribed to just one at a time, *lake* or *woods*, *dirt* or *bear* — as if any of them knew what terror a bear was — and if they claimed to, then I made them take back their claim, and if one would not, then I swore he better, or else in my rage I would take that boy out to the lake, let the deep-swallowed shapes teach him better truth.

The only common trait shared among all the foundlings was their veneration of my wife, who walked every day among their number. The children most like our foundling followed behind her, pleading for her attention. Each wanted to show her some trick of memory, some learned thing, or else a physical feat meant to impress her, and she only rarely was, as she did not remember how to be impressed. She did not know enough of what there was in the world to feel one way or another about what she saw, to know what was better than what, and without memory there could be no right emotions, and of course she had refused what memories she had been given. The foundlings tugged at the hems of her skirts, dirtied them with their fat fingers, then their faces, pressed in close, cheeks against cloth, begging for her touch, for her kiss, for her milkless breasts, and still she did not know what it meant to be a mother, what it had meant to her to be a mother to this child, this one made many brothers.

Mother: Once it was the title of her highest ambitions, and now it became only more mystery. Despite her interest, she did not know who to be, what person these children wanted when they called her by this name, and when their frustration turned to hungry anger, always I was there to intercede, dragging them from off her body, untwisting their fingers from her pulled hair, handling them all more roughly than I wished, and so again, so again.

Back in the house, combing her long white hair—hair that never changed back, even after her fever receded—she asked me what they wanted from her, and I could not tell her, could not explain what I believed, a story I had made for myself: that each wanted to be chosen, to be made the one to be mothered.

I said, Give them nothing yet.

There are too many, I said, and you already once gave so much.

She nodded, smiled, patted my hand, but did not do what I wanted most, did not *remember*: not the first foundling, nor the ache that preceded him, the destruction of the first house that followed.

I said, If you were to fall in love with this many children, what worse thing might you do in their wake?

What wrong thing might we?

As I put her into her bed that night, tucking her slenderness beneath her blankets—my movements tender at last in my oldest age—she said, I want the boys to come live with us.

She said, Boys do not belong in the woods. Boys belong here, in the house.

I shook my head, stroked her hair. Where will they all fit? I asked.

The woods are big enough to hold them, I said. Let them stay in the woods.

She yawned, and then she said, We can always make more house.

She said, We will find a way to take them from the woods, and we will make them each a room in which to live, and in each room a bed for every boy, until the house is exactly the size our family needs the house to be.

Her eyes glimmered, captured the same sad light they did when the fingerling died, when all the other pregnancies that followed ended upon our sheets, ended there until there was the stain that would not come out of those threads.

We can always make more house, she said, until the house is big enough.

T HE RANKS OF THE FOUNDLINGS swelled, their unparented variety now often violent without check: Here was a son that took my side instead of his mother's, dragging some smaller, fairer version of himself across the forest, both boys bloody and beaten.

Here came another, carrying a stick sharpened into a spear, a smile carved into a smirk.

Here a third, one fist full of a rock chipped sharp, marked with the makings of the scalps worn ragged around his waist.

All these children, worse than I'd imagined, and then, fleeing from their brothers, those others more gentle, less prone to violence or at least less capable of carrying it out, and as I hid in the brush and the bramble I saw that there were perhaps three tribes forming loosely, banding together to parent themselves in the absence of better versions of ourselves. Each grouping had only the barest of identities, shifted and still mutable, and while it took my wife longer to see them I had no such difficulties. I observed our memories made flesh again, and as they returned some of them were killed again, and afterward more came to take their place, to become new killers or else again the victims, and while they were greater in number they were lesser in shape, just as the animals I'd trapped and skinned had returned, poorer for having crossed my path just once, and if this time it was not a bear that provided that mechanism then I did not know what else.

The foundlings were not all of one kind: The first were almost as the foundling I knew, their features taken from that face that held no relation to our own, to those of their supposed mother and father. That face was the foundling's from his theft and transformation until his sixth birthday and the scarring of his face, and now it was easier for me to recognize its origins: Under his boyish skin, there was the face of the bear, high and sloped, with a squat nose, a mouth filled with too-early teeth.

Soon after these came other foundlings, more like the one I had known but lacking the wide range of the first: These all shared the same face, or closer to it, their variations of a smaller order, all just different ages of the remade foundling's face, so much like my wife's, remade as such after his scarring, his injury at my hands. These mother-faced children were bigger, but they were not big: Just as the foundling who came to me in the last days of our dirt was not as grown as his age should have rendered him, so these multitudes were hindered, shaped too small for their older voices, their developing adulthoods.

The last foundlings to appear at the tree line were something other, more raw potential than memory: It was only among their number that I counted some teenagers, and also some near-men as old as I was when I met my wife, before I moved farther past, into the endless years I now inhabited. No matter their age, these were the worst to behold, scarred and half shaped, for what they were made of was too slim to be a person. Some missed fingers, others limbs, even the parts of a face that made it a face instead of some other, dumber appendage.

It was these children that were the most dangerous, violent in their wrongness, and often I found one of their number dead upon the fresh-stomped paths or else one of the other children ended by their hands. Soon I walked the woods always with my shovel so that I might bury these children before my wife saw them — although perhaps she never would have, since she did not venture as far as I did, did not go past the more-adoring children at the woods' edge. It was only I who went deep, who interred again the dead, and who slunk all day through the thickets, searching for what my wife, now ignorant in her innocence, could not search for: the child with the right song, with the full knowledge of the elements, with the combination of the two that might save us.

Often I was sneaky in my observations, but other times fits of coughing gave away my presence, or else my cramps left me immobile upon the forest floor, easy prey for the taking, and while the worst of the foundlings had not yet cornered me in such a state, still I watched them grow braver, approaching, and in their eyes I saw some memory of my own, of the way I felt the first time I stalked toward a still-living deer, trapped in my traps.

My fear then? That one day the foundlings would pass the threshold of their hesitance, as I myself had when confronted with that thrashing buck, all those years ago.

T HE RULE THAT PROTECTED US inside the house, upon the dirt around it: Despite their growing numbers, the foundlings still could not leave the woods. At dusk I observed how they withdrew deeper into the woods, hiding far from the tree line, but still I often lay awake, wrapped in my blankets beside my wife's bed, listening for the day the foundlings found some way to overcome their reluctance, as the bear eventually had.

But then one night I heard a new sound instead, a humming made by many voices, far off in the dark: not a song but rather a single note, thrummed out of their many throats, one I recognized, remembered.

This single note, possessed by all? I thought perhaps it was the last note of the song the foundling had used to raise me, a tone able to restart my heart upon the floor of the first house: What they hummed, it was not nearly that song entire, but if they had one note now, then perhaps they would produce more later, and although I knew better I went out of the house and back onto the dirt, back down the path to the woods, and what I saw there was only the empty darkness between the trees, filled not with bodies but with this sound, a child fragmented into noise, and upon my knees I closed my eyes before the buzzing hum, and from the dirt side of the tree line I let it stain me with its promise.

What day was it when my wife and I returned to the tree line together, still hand in hand, as we had taken to walking? What hour was it when we found the woods choked full with children, with all the possibilities of her child, made here into an army of flesh roiling at the tree line, no longer clothed in the white garments they had made from what we had buried, instead pressed naked at the edge of the trees?

What memories we had buried were exhausted now, consumed by what had come after, and still my wife wanted to go to them, cried out as I held her back, because my wife did not see what I saw.

Wanting again to mother, she saw only their nakedness, heard only their cries for her, for any other mother that might appear. I saw and heard that too, but I keened also what waited behind those fronted foundlings, the bear-children, the child-bears, the stained-mouth children who had fashioned their own clothes from a material that could only be their brothers, dead somewhere in the wood and now skinned, and how I gagged to spy it, and this was no way for a mother to see her children, no way for children to act in front of their mother.

It took all the strength left upon my old bones to drag my wife from that tree line, thrashing against my sick grip when the foundlings began to wail, when they cried to her, calling out not the single syllable of her true name, which only I still used, but the joined sounds of her maternal title, the one she once wished to be called instead.

My easily exhausted wife went limp in my arms, and I lifted her off the dirt, carried her away from the woods. Inside the house she fought me again, and I fought her too, dragged her through our rooms, her wrists in my wrists and her legs kicking out, kicking away at every table, at every other furniture, until all surfaces along our path toppled, spilled their contents, filled the house with the shatter of their breakage. When I reached the bedroom, I pushed her inside, and before she could turn back I shut the door and set my weight against it, and when I had it steady I turned my key in the lock, locked her in that room as she had once locked me.

I set my mouth against the door's thick plank, and through the wood I said, You say you are their mother, but you do not even remember their first face.

You do not remember where their faces come from, and they are not yours.

I said, They were never your children. Not these.

I said, Your son is dead.

We buried him, I said, and despite these ghosts he has not come back.

She cried at the door, her voice so close I could feel its vibration in the wood beneath my cheek. She said that she did remember, that she was trying to remember them all.

She said, You told the story wrong, deceived me, hid me from what was mine.

She said, We had so many children, more than you said, and now I want to love them all.

No, I said. No. We had one, and you had one, and both are gone.

Her long motherhood was again upon her, half recalled, and want overwhelmed her, made her some senseless animal, banging and banging against the inside of the door, this trap with which I meant to hold her.

And then the banging stopped.

And then it did not resume.

And then when I opened the door, the bedroom was empty of everything except some tiny wind, blowing through the open window, rustling the curtains across the frame.

And then I had lost her again, because by the time my slower gait returned me to the tree line already I was too distant to do anything but watch as the foundlings parted ranks for her to pass, as they closed that same breach against me: Before me my wife was consumed by the churning crowding of her new foundlings, taken away within a deadly scrum from which she did not return.

MEMORY AS NEW MONTHS SPENT alone: To again be without companionship, except for the ranks of foundlings waiting at the tree line, whose stern bodies would no longer let me pass, and who would not bring me word of my wife, no matter how I begged. To again live in a world of unfaithful wives, a world where mothers chose their children over their husbands. To complain aloud and to no one of this unfairness, to pretend that there was no deeper person in her than what I gave her back, and yet, and yet.

To admit that no matter how I wanted her to be my wife first, still she had not been just mine, not since the moment of our first conception, all those years ago.

To admit defeat, because she never would be mine alone, not ever again, and it was I who had failed to join her, to become some true father to complement her endless motherhood, instead remaining only her husband, that insufficient shape to which always I stubbornly clung.

FROM MY STATION ON THE dirt I kept my vigil, watching for my wife's return from just outside the woods. Whenever I was not weeding our garden or keeping straight our house or maintaining some other part of what world I had been left to steward, then I would return to my chosen spot, close enough to toss the foundlings whatever fruits and vegetables had ripened that day, and each time I fed them I grimaced to watch their hunger grow, but if there was never enough to feed them all, then what other option existed but to provide for some? Afterward, I laid my old bones upon the hard dirt, then waited, waited and watched as they resumed their previous activities, their actions as varied as their faces, their shifted shapes. I memorized the different foundlings that came to the edge of the woods, the ones that kept me from walking beneath its trees, and again I made some catalogue or listing, some roll call unscrolling — and by their differences I knew I named them, even if I had not meant to.

In one foundling, I heard my wife's laugh and, in another, her sigh, some exclamation.

—

And in this foundling, I saw my wife's features most complete, the boy's face like her face, her raven hair long and flowing upon his shoulders.

And in this foundling, her touch, smoothing back the hair of a brother covered in mud and dirt, hungry and hurting, for what food there was was never enough.

And in this foundling, a game I remembered her teaching him, as she had been taught, as he now taught the others.

And in this foundling, a voice like my wife's, singing some snatch of the song I sought. And in this one, some other part, and in this one, a third.

And in this foundling, a look like she had given me, like she gave me often, a look that could mean one or a dozen things, and how it pained me to remember each one, and also them all.

And in this foundling, I saw the bear, her long limbs, her dense muscles, and I saw her apartness, her knowledge that she had given up much to become what she was. I saw this and more, all on the face of one child, who could not understand from what lamentations he was made.

And in this foundling, an angry lesson, scarred into a face burned not here but somewhere far above us, far behind. A face never resung into beauty, belonging to this boy holding down one of his brothers, poking fingers into the younger boy's eyes and nose and mouth. He pinched and folded the flesh of the other's face ugly as his own, and even then he did not stop, even though I cried out to him, even though I pleaded from the dirt, and as always it was as if my words could not cross the thin border between my domain and theirs, and as always it was only as if.

And in this foundling, the kindness of the mother, rocking some smaller child to sleep, cooing all the while, as if mere sound were enough to wish the wicked world away.

And on this foundling, a suit of skin, torn free from another brother, left to wander more naked than naked. And how the skin was sewn with hair. And how it was stained with his brother. And how it kept the foundling warm, so that while the others shivered in the almost dusk, this newly clothed killer stood tall and proud, stupid and unafraid, despite all the world around him, the cold and the tired conspiring to bring him low.

And in this foundling: again, the bear, and now more of her in each new brother.

And so in this one: clawed hands at the end of too-long limbs.

And in another: a hump of muscle twisting his back, giving strength to shoulders and fists.

And in another: a mouth so filled with teeth the lips couldn't fit over what they contained, that jutting sharpness.

And in another: a body covered with snarling fur, thicker than any yet seen, but not thicker than what was yet to come.

And in this foundling, again more of the first: His high, lilted voice. His strange way of standing, cocked sideways, unsure upon his legs. His small hands, his crowded teeth. His hair, thick

and curled, like no one else's, at least no man's. His way of playing, often alone, often at some distance, as if every game required
no other player, and also his eyes, dark and accusing, set in a
dozen and then two dozen heads, all looks landing on me, lingering hard and long and suspicious, and it was no mystery to me
that these gazes remained unfooled, untricked by what gentler
old man I had tried to become, had pretended I had.

I kept one last watch at the edge of the woods, and when morning came still there was no sign of my wife, just these dozens
of worsened children, and again they refused to part, to make
way for me to enter. Even the smallest were like standing stones
against me, and the oldest shook their sticks and lifted their fist-
sized rocks, barked threats, and there was no peaceful way to
pass their barricade. I stepped back, gathered my breath, then let
loose nearly all the sound I had in me, emptied it against their
own loud voices until they were culled into silence, until all the
air was mine.

Every eye was watchful upon me, and to their attention I said, I
am coming through you, and then I am going to my wife, to bring
her back or else to stay at her side.

I said, You will not stop me.

I said, I love her and am her true husband, the only one there
ever was, and the truth of that will grant me passage against you,
all you ghosts.

The foundlings did not speak then, my bravado provoking no
response from either their brightest and oldest, nor from their
youngest, those who might not know better than to speak to one
such as me. And smartly so: for silence was a better answer than
words, and a harder one to take.

I was disappointed by this result but I had hardly expected

more, had been foolish to hope: Mine was not the power of voice, had never been that.

My power, always it was something else, and it was a thing more terrible than even the worst awfulness these shades had imagined. And as they would not give me what I wanted, so now my anger would be brought upon them without further warning, a sudden storm from unclouded sky.

ONG AGO, I GIRDED MYSELF against the woods with an armor of fur, with a trap chained to my skin, with one knife upon my belt and another swallowed into my heart. Now there were no such arms available, and so when I returned to the house I had to search again for some other method to clothe myself, some other way to make my intentions known. Most of what was in the house was mere domestics, but in our closets there hung one apparel that might serve, that had served me first, on my best day: My wedding suit, white as it was once white, remade again by my wife's memories, its original purpose as forgotten by her as anything else.

I stripped naked, scrubbed my body in the boil of the last bucket of water, brought earlier from the lake. Washing myself with that captured gallon, I could feel my capacity for transformation in its wetness, dormant but never gone, and when I was clean I shaved my face bare, and when I was shaved I took my wife's scissors to my hair, cut it in the ancient fashion of our wedding year. I trimmed my nails with the same blades, then brushed my teeth, scrubbed at their squares with my fingers, with soda and salt.

Then the suit, then the pants and the shirt and the jacket, then the tie that my hands had nearly forgotten how to knot, that took too many efforts to hang right.

I did all the things I did the morning of my wedding, and when I was finished I was as close as I could come to what I once was, and what sad and sallow shadow I made, and in our mirror I saw all my ruin made more obvious by its scrubbing: My cataracted eye, hung low in its socket; the many scars of forgotten origin. How my one shoulder lifted lower than the other, how my one leg dragged so that even standing still I looked to limp. How even with the same haircut I did not have the same hair I'd had, its peak upon my forehead higher and thinner than when I was young.

What I saw in the mirror was my dying, and how at last it was near, so near I could always smell it, could put my fingers to my skin and feel it moving beneath, beneath and also within.

I was failed father, failing husband, failure in every role, and still I went on, up and out of that house and toward the tree line, my dragging steps dredging the dusty dirt, that ground bereft of the rain my wife forgot to add to her last world, our deepest house. As I walked I corrected my gait until my hips ached, then I let my body move again in the manner its turned nature wanted, ankle sideways, arms outward, good eye leading my leaning face, pointing me toward what I knew awaited me beneath the first trees, a roaring column of her worst children, some naked and howling, bear-faced or not, and all united in how they would not let me pass.

To recognize the impossibility of hiding my approach from the foundlings, so not to try.

To keep my gaze pointed past their small faces and their wild expressions, into the long woods beyond.

To maintain that the foundlings were no children, no prize, only horded distraction.

To make believe — to make a belief — that I could prevail against them, and that if I did I might find now some recent-made cave farther into the woods, a cave not there before my wife came to dig it from the earth.

And as I crossed the tree line the foundlings fell upon me, and in their haste one another too, their sound swarming, and together they punished me with their sharp bodies, and then they ripped my wedding suit, and then all the man that lay beneath it.

MY FLESH, MARKED WITH A topography of anger.

My hair, torn from my scalp in clumps, my scalp torn.

My eyes, poked and pried, until both the good eye and the cloudy saw only tears, a lasting sparkling.

My ear twisted, then a finger pulled back and back and broken, then enough of that, enough damaging the surface; then the tearing of my skin, the breaking of what was within, and then my crying out, my begging for mercy, mercy, and how I did not deserve it, and then my saying my wife's name, saying it almost voiceless for there was so little voice left, begging that from wherever she had gone she might remember me and so call off the children she had made, and then, at last, something new to hear, something come through the growls and screams, the hackled roars of these piled children, a sound heard not in my good ear, but in my bad one: A series of notes, not quite like a song, coming from beneath the floor of the woods, up and out of the earth, a sound high pitched at first, and then a noise so low its tone was felt only in my vibrating organs, my jumping spilling blood.

The foundlings unpiled themselves from atop my bones, stood

to howl some response, stamping their feet against what frustration the sound brought, and while they were occupied elsewhere
I tried to look down and around at my twisted shape, my broken structures, then struggled to turn over, to put hands and feet
beneath me—and despite my felt efforts, no change in position happened, no muscles responded. All my bones seemed unconnected
to any other, and perhaps they were, for when my right hand and
then my left hand returned to my control, all they found was blood,
and then everywhere I placed my knees and elbows and head was
blood too, and the worst pain was across my belly, and when I put
one hand there it slipped right through, into the strung-out hurt of
my stomach, the long guts surrounding.

At last I was finished, at last this body was going to fail and fail
until it stopped failing, and how for a moment this thought ran a
smile across my split lips, my broken teeth, my torn tongue, for
some ever-larger part of me no longer wanted to be the one who
went on but only the one who had stopped, and yet there was some
slim hope left, one cowardly path left untaken: If I could turn away
from my wife and leave the woods, if I could make it across the dirt
upon my knees and my belly, if I could crawl the length of the dock
to drop myself in the water, then I would again become the squid,
relieved of my injuries, changed for the last time. I pulled my cowardice forward, felt what was loosed within me dragging against
the unpacked earth, felt my insides getting dirty in hollows no longer protected by skin and fat, and then vomit spilled upward, filled
my mouth and my nose, and some similar stinking liquid leaked
out of my stomach, its punctured sac.

Then the sound again, and then after it the noise, and then the
sound and the noise, together, and yes, then at last a song, and yes,
and yes, and who sang it where, and I did not know, could not see
anymore, and what was not pain was numb, and what was not deaf

heard only that song, and then foundlings everywhere, all around, their hands upon me, and me not looking, not able to look and happy for it, for what more did I want of their deadly differences?

A dozen arms lifted me, a dozen more moving under to carry all of me, even the parts escaping the shattered container of my body, all those blood-let organs, and with each step the foundlings took I cried out, and the movement of so many hands made an uneven gurney, but they did not slow nor answer whatever unintelligible queries I tried to make, and anyway I asked only to lose consciousness, to fall toward the buzzing light awaiting, but always I was tasked to witness, to remember, and so I bore it, and from atop their hands I looked through the trees and into that wife-made sky, always before empty, and there I saw some stars appear against the dusky bowl, and I knew those new stars by their old names; for they were the stars my wife had called down from our sky all those longest years before, that had fallen through the lake and into the black below, and in them I saw some letters of that ancient alphabet restored, the old stories, and while they were not complete still I recognized their shapes, sky-bear and tall-tree, gold-crown and lake-whale, first-father and ever-mother —

And then my sight was gone, and then there was no more sky, only some more constrained space, and even through my blindness, some transition from light to darkness, from level to sloped. And then being carried through that darkness, down into it. And then stretches of time not stopping, unmarked by anything but the steady breathing of those many foundlings carrying me onward, and when one tired he was replaced by another, and on the back of this swarming litter I descended without stoppage, all the wreck of me carried as one thing, if a spill could be so carried, rushed onward, down into darker dark, stronger song.

A FTER THAT LONG PORTAGE, THERE was again light, but the sights that returned with it were nothing I saw with my eyes, although I opened them too, useless as they were.

What did I see then, with that other gaze? Ceiling at first, and ceiling only, from where I lay suspended, belly up atop the foundlings, now crowded close together, a press of bodies below me, keeping me aloft. We had entered a cave, and the cave was like the one my wife and I had lived in while I built our house.

To the foundlings, I said, Enough.

I said, Please, you have carried me far enough.

They had carried me, and also the tune of the song, and the song was louder here than it was in the woods or the passages we journeyed down to reach wherever here was. Now I heard how they voiced it without inflection, without tone, and yet all the notes were correct, although correct as opposed to what I did not know, sure only of their correctness. I did not think they would hear me speak, not over the volume of the song, and also of the sound, these two separate but similar things now loud together, loud even through my deafness, which like my blindness had not mitigated, only been made different, so that while it had not been healed still I could hear, and so the foundlings did too, and in one motion they lowered my body to the floor.

By that light I looked upon my body, a glance so brief it could only survey the vast damage, the irreconcilable nature of my wounds, not sickness alone but also the crude angers of these foundlings. There was no saving myself that I saw, and so no reason to withhold any effort. I forced myself to stand, felt the breaks in my body shift around my new stance, and then I gathered my spilled self up into my arms, forced it rudely back through the hole in my belly, which no longer bled. I closed my eyes, breathed in, smelled the copper and cordite of my pains, and when I opened my eyes again, then the song stopped.

Now there was more air in the room, more unbreathed breaths remaining, and soon I saw all there was, gathered in that gloom: All the foundlings, wood-sprung, crowded close in all their wrongness, any slivers of rightness remembered encased in fault and waste and never. On their circled faces were formed all the expressions that together might have combined to make one lost boy's face, but once separated those features made no sense, nothing any whole person would mistake for the same articulation, and yet I knew my wife had so mistaken, and in their swarmed faces—their hundreds of faces, arrayed in every direction, from wall to wall, point to point in the darkness—I almost missed hers, hung there in front of me, a glowing moon of skin set atop her long neck, her graceful shoulders, her slim body not standing above the foundlings but sitting among them, rested in some rocking chair, so much like the one I had made her that it returned pain to my body, which had been numb to such sensation—or rather, pain returned to me, floating around and through, my body nerveless, barely present.

My wife rocked, but no child sat upon her lap.

My wife, she had tested every child there, but none had fit, no one child matching that weight she missed without admitting her missing, that voice she craved without knowing what it would sound like when next it was heard. These foundlings were her wishes, her griefs manifested in all their glory and blame, and as she stood into the space between me and them I saw in her revealed shape the return of the scorched wife, the burned woman I had found upon reaching the deepest house, and for a moment I startled at the sight, for I realized that in that cave I had expected to find not a wife at all but rather a bear, a bear afire, made from the woman my wife had been.

And what had averted that fate? What had kept her from what change befell the wife before her, the foundling's mother, my long adversary?

Perhaps only the fire within, which would abide no clothes upon her, and perhaps no fur either.

Away from my stories, she had become herself again, the woman she had arced toward whenever I was not there to tell her whom I wanted her to be; and in her absence I had also moved toward this limited man I was now, this best man I could be.

My wife's heat blazed immense, and if I'd still had sweat within me it would have burned away, wicked from the flapping of my skin. My armful of myself dried, shrank in my hands, my mouth parched, my nostrils singed with the smell of their hair. I turned my face away, felt the prickle of her heat follow my cheek, and then I righted my gaze, held her eyes steady as she held mine: Here she was, and here I was before her, drawn as always to this woman, these women she had been, pulled through time and memory, through those long bodies of the world.

My wife, I said, and the heat from her licked at my lips, dried my voice.

I said, I have been no husband to you, and the fire ate my words, so that I had to wet my mouth, reloose my tongue.

My wife, I said, I have been no husband, and no father, but you have been a mother to these children — and that was the whole truth of it. As broken and bad as these foundlings might be, they were hers if she wanted them, and she had gathered them close, had accepted the mothering even of the most awful: Not the memories of me, or of our first lost son — my son, my fingerling — but of this foundling, this one whom she had not birthed but for whom she had done all else, had nursed, had taught, had swaddled and sang to, and it was in him that she was best to be found, in this person made lovely to her even if never to me.

Now in this cave, all the foundling's aspects were gathered, real and otherwise, and I did not doubt she could see them all, all the possibilities of his past and present, his future.

My wife's skin, black already, blackened again, and as she moved her head around me I heard the crinkle of her flesh, again like the pages of a book, a story crackling.

I knew I could not smell the smoke that filled the room, no longer had any sense of smell, and then through the smoke my wife said, Time and time again you have told me about our children, about all the children you see, but I do not see what you see.

Her face so and close, yes, a whiff of her old perfume, hidden behind history or else only a scented memory, and no right sense. She was so old now — we were both so old — but still I found her beautiful, and here, in this beauty, I always would be arriving, however long delayed: I did not know how much deeper the world went, how many more caves beneath caves there were, but there was no longer any distance I would not follow her, no unlit chambers that could hide her fire, and always I would seek her through the darkness, and always I would deliver my body bowed beneath my awe at what and who she was, by what more she had become and was becoming:

Here were the children I wanted to have with her or, if not the ones I dreamed, then the dreams I deserved, right for what world I had made.

Here was the foundling, now one made many, and on each one's lips was a song or part of a song, the songs she sang of them before they came and also after.

Here was the foundling, her mothering of him: our parenting that I had barely joined, and then my withdrawal from that arrangement, its continuation in my absence.

Here was her deep house, which I had burned in my frustration.

Here were her great stairs, left to lead me through the black, even if I was too much a coward to follow.

Here was my wife, scorched and sad and forgetful, and here was me, her husband, supplicant and penitent, and how far she'd had to go to get me to follow her right, so that I might arrive at the place where I could at any time have come more easily with less pain for her and for all others.

For all my life, I thought that she was the receptacle into which I would put some seed of mine, make the family I wanted, but it was I who was the empty vessel, carved stubborn as stone, as unburnable as the moon, ready at last to be filled with the *fire* and with the *song*, and these last two elements were weaved so deeply into the hidden magic of the world that I had forgotten to count them among my numbers, although all my life they had been there to make us: And then the foundlings sang, Let there be *fire*, and then there was fire beneath the earth.

MY WIFE PUT HER HAND upon my face, said, I remember you now. You have righted yourself, fixed your face from out your beard, cut away the wrong hair.

She said, You changed without me, and I forgot how to recognize you through the changes.

And what was there to do but to agree?

My wife raised her free hand, placed it on my other bare cheek, and then her body burst black inside its flame, those flicking tongues white-blue, then hotter colors, colors hued indescribable, and the stone floor of the cave heated too, and all the foundlings cried out, their ghostly range of voices so narrow, so similar. My pooled and pooling blood sizzled, evaporated, and then I was falling, and still my wife gripped my face, held me from off my knees. She lifted me straight, pulled me to her, and then the flames were through my skin, inside my open body, razing away the last shreds of my wedding suit, and still I could not look at her, ashamed as I was of my old and broken shape, dying grotesque.

My wife, she took my slipping guts from out my hands, pushed them back in through my open belly, and then she said, Husband.

She said, Husband, I remember you.

She said, I remember singing you your vows, and then her hands were inside me too, so horrible and hot, what her fever must have felt like, the halls of memory enflamed, and still the fire spreading, spreading. I opened my eyes to see her, black before me in the dark and the flame, the surface of her shape again the negative of the one I had better known, and when she removed her hands she left me open, and then she moved against and around me in the fire, her long legs making circling steps, and in the fire she began to sing, and as the fire and the song grew it became a furnace, and we were in it together, and the foundlings too, the vastness of them, their child-faces pressed close, and now like us they were even less flesh and bones than before, and in their difference and their disarray they came faster and faster, and from each of their lips my wife took one note, and when the child was soundless he moved into the fire, and then the fire moved into me, into her, into us, and how full I got, how fast moving my thoughts, like a clock ticking full of futures new and unlikely and somehow possible, and how lovely my wife's song was, and how long before it was over I knew there would be no foundlings left, that it was in them that my wife's story was stored, the before and after of my leaving her, kept in her true child, the one I had buried in her last woods, and what she had waited for in her house was not me and my story but her *son*, returned to her and by the woods restored, as another woods had restored so many of the other lives I had failed to steward or to groom, and the song my wife sang was the finest I had ever heard, but it was not the song I had searched for.

This song, it did not restore me, but that was no longer why I had come, and no more would my want be to go on and on and on, to live without end, a desire that would not have stopped with the

death of my body or my children's or their children's but only with
the extinction of every possible world, so that my end would come
at the termination of all things, that last threshold of possibility.

No more, I said, begged with my mouth filling with fire, my
eyes and my hands and my stomach and lungs filled with the
same.

No more was enough, I begged, and more than I deserved.

Only after the last of the foundling had passed between us was my
body closed and my wife's opened, enclosing me, drawing me in.
It was not the love we'd had, but it was enough, and there at the
bottom of the world I moved my broken body against hers, and in
that cave I once more gave half a child into her, where our many
wants might meet the half a child she had left, the memory of a song,
and yes, throughout our coupling she sang, and it was a new
song, made from the song that had made the fingerling and all
his failed brothers and sisters, that had made the new moon and
made the deep house and the deeper house and this deepest house,
its dirt and lake and woods, its foundlings, its cave beneath them
all, buttressed by the bones of the world, made a vault or else a safe
haven, so that no matter how many levels collapsed above us still
our child might somewhere be protected from the mistakes of its
parents.

A FTER OUR RETURN TO THE house, we resumed for a time our lives together, as husband and wife.

My wife's body paled again, and this new color lasted, her skin now flush only with her songs, a music employed to sing back the world we had known and also to better it: A sun rose in the sky the week after our return, or at least some convincing illusion of one, and that night, after it set, a moon followed its unrestrained arc. Clouds came later, and then rain falling, and then grass poking through the dirt, although from what seeds, from where? I did not know, did not ask. No longer did I need to know all the seats of power. It was enough that my wife's songs added to what we had, and anyway I was not restored as she was, and so my old and tired body had not the strength to fight. At night we slept in a bed together — a bed of wood again and not of stone — but in the mornings I often arose coughing and sore to find her already gone, hanging again some photographs upon the wall or else rebuilding the nursery I had turned into my den. During the day she gardened, and as she gardened she sang to our child, the one growing within, made below the earth but destined to live upon it.

This time, there was no boredom at the slow progress of her pregnancy, the weeks of slimness nor the first small bulge that followed. Together, we touched and listened and sang, my rough and toneless voice doing its best below the beauty of her right one, and while only rarely had I sung with her before, now I did at every chance, whenever my throat was not too ravaged, and for less than a year, this was our life.

That near year, it was not without its sorrow, and its passing did not forgive us or help us to forget what we had done, but it was good enough for me to accept my fate, the fate of this place, the last of all the world I would ever see, and even as it was improved by measures, still I knew it would prove temporary.

It was the last world for me, but not for my wife, made young again, and not for our child, who with my wife I had determined must escape, must inherit what first home we had made, to make of it as she would or else choose to leave it behind, to return to that country from which her parents had embarked, the one on the other side of the lake, across the mountains, that busy land where we were born, all those many worlds ago.

My wife and I first denied the coming of the end, but the signs became manifest, multiplied. Even with her restored song and her many feats that followed, it seemed this last place was doomed to fall, and so it was the woods that failed first, their trees growing leafless with the advance of days, then rotting, toppling to the ground. There was no life there, and no bear to make more, to roar right the shapes it required, and eventually not even any cave, that hollow having collapsed some months into my wife's pregnancy, after it became obvious she would not return. The lake was similarly diminished but faded more slowly, drying up with every day I spent on the land instead of swimming beneath its surface as my next nature desired me to do. From the shore, I sometimes watched the fingerling-fish flash through the water, plentiful without my culling but seemingly senseless too, now only animals that I pretended I felt no kinship to, no responsibility for.

With the trees leaf-bare and the water dropping, an ill-tasting wind began to blow across the dirt, eroding its surface into the air, and already that new sun was dimming, that new moon's orbits growing less straight, more heavy looking upon the sky, and soon there would be no reason to stay here, and perhaps no way. My wife had made the shape we needed for our story, and now our story was ending, and so also its world.

Memory as last conversation: To wait in my chair upon the porch, old and tired, bones aching and eyes heavy, for my now-round wife to return from her gardening behind the house. To allow her to sit down beside me, to take my hand in hers. To smile but to wait for her to speak, then to listen so close to her words, the favorite song of her soft speech, and then to hear her say that it was time for us to leave, to take our child from this place.

My wife then, she was not exactly herself—not the self I had known—but she was some new woman like her and just as easy to love.

My wife, she said: I do not remember the world you spoke of, that you told me was once like this one, but I want to see it, and if I am the reason it was destroyed, then I want to be the method by which it might be rebuilt.

With her hand in my hand, with her eyes on mine, she said, I want our child to have everything we wanted to give a child, and to give her our world together.

Come with me, she said, and for a moment I thought that she knew my plans, but then she continued, and I saw that my latest secret — last of them all — was yet mine alone.

She stood, lifted me from my chair, and then she said, Come with me and help me get ready, for there is much left to do and so little time to do it.

And how she was right, and also wrong, for time was not what she thought it was, in her new youth, nor what I had thought it was in mine, passed so very long ago.

I did not know what my wife would find when she reached the surface, nor truly how well she might weather the journey upward, climbing the great stairs and pushing through the black only to arrive at the terrible truth of the deep house, the rent and ruined rooms of that palace that had held the treasures of her person.

I did not know if the surface above burned or bloomed or if there were any walls remaining of our first house, any chimney still allowing guesses as to where walls once stood, might go again.

Perhaps she would reach the surface to find the way impassible and would not be able to climb out of the earth without more destruction, without carving her way forward, and what then, and what would that do to what unmarked mother she had become?

Perhaps, perhaps, and no answers anyway.

There were just the two of us now, and also the one coming, and most often we were quiet and simple with each other, and in bed that night I laid behind my wife, put my hand atop her belly, and as our baby kicked within I asked her about the song the foundling had sung over me, in the moment after my heart attack. Did she remember that song? Had she taught it to him? Did she still have it to sing?

My wife could not see my face, and I did not permit her to turn around, to face my face while she answered. I did not want her to see my expression, to see what ugly thing hope was doing there, to my twisting lips, my twitching cheeks.

I said, Answer me where you are, or else don't.

My wife, she pressed back into me, patting my hand on her belly with her hand, and then she said, What if it was the other that restored you? That saved you when you needed him most?

No, I said. It was not him.

And yet! And always, and no matter. All that was ended, and this too.

EARLY STILL, ON THE MORNING of our scheduled departure: I left our bed in the chilled hour before the dawn, careful not to wake my wife. I took one last look at her, at the swelled curves of her body, at her face more precious to me than ever before, except maybe at the very first. When I had seen all I could hope to see, then I slipped out of the house and down to the lake.

At the edge of the dock, I removed my clothes, folded them onto the slats, the sung boards made to resemble the other dock above, the one I had made with my own hands. I felt the dew upon those planks, wiggled my toes against that damp, then shivered at the breeze goosebumping the scarred and folded leather of my skin.

Those scars were my palace as the deep house was my wife's, as the woods and the cave were the bear's, as much as any other part of my flesh, another version of my story lashed from my ankle to my back to my shoulder, to my chest and my face and my hands, and now I was leaving all of them behind.

I had told my wife what I had done and what it had made me, and still she took me back.

I believed she loved me again, and because she loved me, I had kept one more secret plan, this tucked-away mercy.

Memory as stretched moment, as elastic time, as always for me the moments have been: To know that I had made all the journeys I could, or would. To believe that my wounds had left me mostly unfit for marriage, for fatherhood, for any world less simple than this one, and my wife and our coming child deserved better, because despite my softening I believed it was better to have no husband than one like me.

To imagine my wife might have said this was not for me to decide.

To agree in principle, while still rejecting her claim, while choosing not to give her the chance to voice it.

When I dared delay no longer, I flexed my body beneath my old skin, felt its sure response despite its many creaks and popping cracks: This man was going to die, but the squid the man could choose to be might live some time longer, at least until the lake was dry, just dust dispersing, blown upon the last wind. In that water awaited the only other I had not forgiven, and before this deep-sunk world was ended I wanted whatever there could be between us, between my last shape and his, even if this thing I would be wanted nothing so grand, needed nothing but what could be provided by instinct, by hunger and rutting. I hoped that within that simplicity was left some space, a slimness where the last of a man might control what a squid would be, what it became—and then I felt the first heat of the morning's sun—and then I was running for the end of the dock, the last running I would ever do, and as I reached the edge I leaped—and in the air I felt some catch in my throat, a black thread long swallowed, a black hair tugged taut and then snapping — and what an awful relief it was — and after I hit the water, how horrible it was to still be *me*, how I had hoped that I would not be, and yet still there I was, always me me me, man as trapper and hunter, as bear-bane, as ghost-killer, as husband failed, father-failure, squid and —

— memory as mid-shift, mid-sentence, mid-sound: To be beneath the light-dappled surface but not yet deep. To turn back and see a shape standing on the edge of the platform, tall and heart-proud against the sky, then tumbling forward into the water, a falling pile of bones and skin and regret, what that shape was always going to become, no matter how well it tried to love, no matter how badly it had most often failed to do so, and as it fell it broke the surface of the lake —

— and in the lake there was water and salt and black fish, blacker eels, and more of each every day. How the fish sustained the eels, and the eels the squid. Getting full and staying full. Sated, satisfied. Then the fish moving inside even as they moved without. Then the squid's body suddenly heavy, until swimming was torture. Then the surface unreachable by any effort, then descending in wide circles, sinking through soundless depths. Then more and more of the black fishes, still each a finger's length, and then more of the eels, longer and wider and heavier toothed.

Then darkness, then blackness — then what was below the blackness, the second layer of blacker black.

Then realizing the blackness moved, was moving, that the blackness had scales, had fins and tails, had voices, saying FATHER, saying FATHER. Voices hungry, unfooled by new shapes, each speaking memories and prophecies.

Voices, many voices, but also only one, and in the deepest of the depths, something else, a mass of flesh and bone sunk earlier to the bottom, now split and torn, now more food for these angrier shapes, and now the squid trapped beside it, held down by their weight, wounded by their biting through the mantle, their scrabbling at armor and shell—

—and still I remembered, although I did not want to, and still I went on, because I was not without my power, not without danger, protected by hook and tentacle and hard beak, and even then the fingerlings were not worried. There were more of them than there were of me, and they were patient, and they were thorough. One day they would consume me, make their new life from mine, from what mine had become, as always they had promised me they would: When they were done with the bear, they would come for the squid, and from me they would take their last strength, and if it happened before the lake dried, still I would be satisfied, because they would be ended too, trapped as I wanted them trapped, given no more entry to the better worlds above, and their future was so short, and the real future was elsewhere, and when I was not only the squid I could see it coming, a prophecy so sure it seemed a final memory, a history already past:

My wife, pregnant upon the great stairs, climbing tall steps in the dark.

My wife, pregnant upon a landing over a chasm, pregnant in the empty halls of the deep house, crying for what had been lost.

My wife, pregnant and expectant, climbing out of the earth and back onto the dirt, where a shattered house stood or did not stand.

My wife, doubled with contractions, singing through the pain to close the sundered dirt, to flatten the land.

My wife, clutching her swelling, delaying the baby so close now; my wife delaying to sing foundations back down into the dirt, singing up walls atop those foundations, singing up roof and windows and doors — and then when the house was ready my wife walking through the front door, clutching at every new rail and corner, pulling herself into a bedroom much like a bedroom she had known, and then lying down upon the same-shaped bed.

My wife, screaming the birth-song she had waited a life to sing entire, her sound beautiful as a bird's, angry as a bear's, and her hands now raising her skirts, now delivering alone this new and howling child, some whole daughter come at last, whom together we had cracked dirt and time in want of, her tiny shape now filling my wife's messy arms, and still the birth-song continuing, creating everything else a child's world might need, beasts and fowl and fish, stars and story and songs, more songs, one song to contain all others, and all of them together still only one, all elements combining to make a world, to give that world a name, to give that name to a child, who might carry it forward, onward into whatever awaited her, whatever other landscape she would make to call her own, and then the past was ending, and then the present began, and then I saw the future just beyond it, everything that happened next, but not to me.

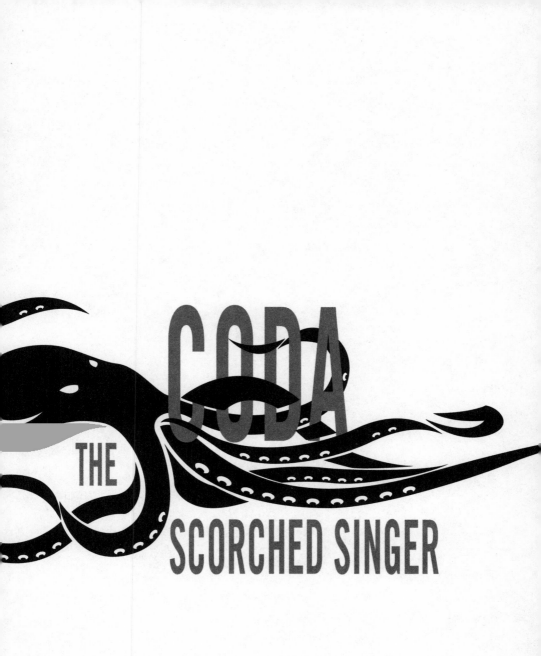

CODA

THE

SCORCHED SINGER

A ND THEN ONE MORNING SHE found a man upon the shore of her lake, floated in from the shallows, his naked body white and rent, his back dug deep enough to expose muscle beneath skin, bone beneath muscle.

She withdrew, then moved closer again. Turning him over, she revealed a face she did not recognize, not from before her long loneliness: One of the man's eyes was cloudy, the other shot with blood, and there was no breath in him, none moving his face and lungs. She shuttered the man's eyes, then closed his mouth, hiding his broken teeth. Everywhere she touched, the man's skin stretched away, its shape tattered, his chest scarred from some multiple cracking wounds, all his other injuries far older than his drowning, left unset or else healed by an ugly method.

She did not investigate further: The man was dead, and that was enough. She had left enough mysteries unsolved, did not need another.

The coming of the man had fouled her lake: What water was once blue and filled with sparkle was now grayed, even blackened out near the center, where some other filth swirled in the slow current. She watched the second shape froth and decided that soon she should make the lake bigger again, so that whatever contaminant this man had brought might be spread thinner.

But first there was the body of the man. She could not decide where to put him, whether to burn his body or else bury it in the dirt near the shore or perhaps up the slope or even farther still, on the other side of the house or in the woods beyond, and while she deliberated she went to the house and stripped the sheets off her bed.

A selfish thought: If the body had drifted back into the lake by the time she returned, then she would pretend him a dream, like the other men she had dreamed in the past few weeks — and then a smile upon her face, because she had almost thought *remembered* instead: Men hunting in the woods, setting traps. Men coming down some long and spiraling stairs. Men banging their fists upon a door hidden in the rock at the far edge of the dirt. But the men she had seen had not been this man, only some other progression of shapes: one a young man, dressed in a white suit; one in his middle years, bearded, dressed in furs; and a third, some aged wanderer, coughing blood into his hands, wiping his fingers on his skinny thighs.

When she was very young there had been another woman who had lived in this house with her, who had cared for her, fed her, clothed her, taught her. That other had passed from the dirt long ago, and later she too had gone away, leaving by an almost-vanished road for a more crowded country, for its tall and sprawling capital. Later she had returned to the dirt by another passage, a blacker escape, and now she was again alone, lonely despite some lingering mysteries, the men in her dreams, and also these few recurring sounds: the laughter of a child, the roar of a bear, the angry words of a father, speaking to someone else, some other woman about to be hurt.

And where had these phantoms come from? Were they waiting here for her return, or had she brought them back with her? And why could she not remember?

The man's body was still beached when she returned to the shore, and now there was another object too, washed up beside him. Something white, flowing in the water.

It was not until she got closer that she saw that floating outline was merely a wrapping come partway undone, a covering for another smaller shape.

It was not until she was almost upon both the new shape and the man's that she recognized the second for what it was: The white shape was a shroud, made of wet and dirty bedsheets, and those sheets matched those she held in her hands, had been put to the same purpose she intended hers, the impermanent preservation of the dead.

This new shape was so small it could only contain a child, and her fingers trembled as she twisted her hands in the sheets and pulled it ashore. The sheets were closed by locking folds, and she undid them one by one, and though she wanted to look away as she opened the last one, she did not.

Inside the shroud was the body of a boy, six or seven years old, or maybe even older—a runt, stunted. A cry caught in her throat as she lifted him out, and then the smell from within the shroud gagged her, transforming her earlier sound into something new, and still she did not look away: The boy had been dead an even longer time than the man, and now his features were collapsed, his face no longer a face, the skull stove-in, the teeth jutted through the softened skin of his lips.

She picked up his hands, found his long fingernails curled into the fleshy pads of his palms, tearing clawed indents, tiny wounds. This was a body damaged by time, by time and by submersion in water — and how long had they been there in her lake, and where had they floated there from? The boy's shape demanded something of her, some consolation, and she did not wish to deny what she felt, had determined to deny herself nothing. She lifted him onto her lap, into her arms, felt his weight upon her, and how he was filled with the lake then, and how when she squeezed him closer that water came out, through his mouth and nose, the other wounds decayed across his flesh.

The water that covered her, it was not all from her lake, and when it flooded her mouth she remembered not everything but something more than she had, or else she almost did. What she remembered was already present in her world: Here too there was already *house* and *dirt* and *woods* and *lake, sun* and *moons*, and yes, *ghosts* too, for what else could account for her dreams? Here there was always *wife* and always *mother*, for she might have been both even if she was neither now, and here there was always *son*, for she had made one of those once too, and before that was *husband* — and even if she could not remember his face she remembered his voice, how tone-deaf he was, how he spoke ceaselessly because like most men he could not sing, and because he could not say anything without too many words.

She was old, in the last of her ages, but she thought she was not stupid, only forgetful.

In the floating blackness she had forgotten all the faces she had known, but now here there were two more, dead in the shallows of the lake she had made for herself and for them, for someone like them — so that when they came for her it would be as if they were already home.

There were many songs inside her, even then.

There was a song for the making of the objects by which a household was furnished and run, the bowls and breadboards and spoons and knives and pots and pans.

There was a song for the waking of a child, and for putting him to bed. There was a song for his birthday, and also for each day in between, each day during which he became different from the day before.

There was a song for making milk, even inside the breast of a barren woman, so that a child might be nursed even though his mother was not his mother.

There was a song for sewing clothing, and another for mending holes in those clothes, because there was exactly one right song for every action, for every desired artifact or outcome, and always it was important to sing the right song at the right time.

There was a song for the making of moons, but it cost so much to sing that it might take years to recover from, because the hole it cut would pool with grief, until nothing else might grow inside that circle.

There was a song for the carving of the earth, but its every note required one piece of herself, something to put where that earth had been, so that the dirt might not collapse. There was no creation from nothing but only from cost, and it was mostly with herself that she might pay.

There was a song for marriage, and another for anniversaries, and another for divorce.

There was a song for sickness, for fever, but it had not saved her when she was sick and fevered.

There was a song for birth, and a song for funerals, and it was the funeral song she sang now as she stacked wood upon the sandy shore, as she stacked the man and the boy upon the wood.

When the pyre was ready, she sang it aflame, then stood watch over the burning bodies. The fire climbed, and as she watched the blaze she fevered and she flamed and she sang the funeral song. And afterward her world grew quiet, and she was quiet in it, sure there was no man or beast left that knew her name, no one that might guess where she had fled or what had happened to her.

She believed herself alone in her world for just that single moment, a moment exactly as long as it was, and then something else splashed from the lake behind.

She turned to look out across the surface of the lake, and then from the water came the loud sound of them, the many where once there was one, and she had forgotten that too, had thought she had left it behind, but then she remembered how it had felt, remembered it now, so many years after it first swam from within her. She listened to the strange speech, and then she put a finger to her lips.

She said, Hush now.

She said, Mother says be quiet, just a little longer.

And then the splashing stopped.

And then the singing began.

ACKNOWLEDGMENTS

MATT BELL IS GRATEFUL TO Ryan Call, Roy Kesey, and Robert Kloss, for their generous feedback; to Aaron Burch, Elizabeth Ellen, Steven Gillis, and Dan Wickett, for their friendship and encouragement; to Bradford Morrow, Carmen Giménez Smith, David McLendon, Jason Diamond and Tobias Carroll, Catherine Chung and Meakin Armstrong, and Kate Bernheimer and Alissa Nutting, for publishing excerpts in *Conjunctions*, *Puerto del Sol*, *Unsaid*, *Vol. 1 Brooklyn*, *Guernica*, and *Fairy Tale Review*; to Bronwen Hruska, Paul Oliver, Meredith Barnes, Rudy Martinez, Simona Blat, and the rest of the team at Soho Press, for their championing of this novel; to Janine Agro, Kapo Amos Ng and Sam Chung for their beautiful design and artwork; to Kirby Kim, for his invaluable advice and advocacy; to Mark Doten, whose belief and ability improved every page; and finally, but first and always, to Jessica, for her love and support.

Too Strange md